ANYWHERE WITH YOU

KAYLEE RYAN

Cover Design: Shanoff Designs
Photographer: Lindee Robinson Photography
Editing: Hot Tree Editing
Proofreading: Deaton Author Services

DEDICATION

To my husband, without you this would not have been possible.

CHAPTER ONE

Allison

"GRAN, THIS IS A BAD IDEA."

"Allie girl, how many times do I have to tell you, I'll be fine? You're only going to be forty minutes away. You need to go, spread your wings, and live your life. I want that for you more than anything."

"But, Gran! We need to stick together, we're a team, the two of us. I hate the thought of someone else taking care of you. That's my job," I counter. I know, I'm being childish, but the thought of leaving Gran alone is breaking my heart. Yes, she'll have a nurse for eight hours a day, but she'll be alone at night. This scares me. Gran suffers from heart disease and diabetes, which makes it hard for her to get around and do everyday things, such as cook and clean. Taking care of these tasks had been my responsibility until the day we found out I had to live in the dorms at the University of North Carolina, UNC for short. I tried to use that as an excuse not to go, but she wouldn't take no for an answer.

"My sweet, sweet girl. I love you for that, but you need this. Ace is there, he misses you. I need you to make a way in this world for yourself. Staying in the dorms is the right decision. You have a lifetime of new experiences waiting for you. The Emersons are just next door, and the nurse will be here seven days a week."

"But—"

"That's enough. Allison, listen to me, you're going to stay in the dorms and live it up, like all the other kids your age. I've watched you give up too many experiences for me, and I won't stand for it any longer. I love you with all my heart, but you need to do this, for both of us."

"Fine, but I'm coming home every weekend to see you," I grumble. Knowing that further arguing will only upset her more.

"Oh, no you don't, missy. You'll come home no more than one weekend a month, and even that isn't necessary. Put yourself first, for once, Allison. Take chances, make mistakes, fall in love," Gran replies at the same time a knock sounds on the door.

"Come in!" I yell.

"Hey, guys, it's just us," Jennifer Emerson says, as she and her husband, Michael, walk into the living room. The Emersons live next door, and also happen to be my best friend Ace's parents. They've helped fill the void of my parents, who passed away in a tragic car accident when I was ten.

"Hey, sis, you all set?" Michael asks me as he pulls me in for a hug. Since the day I moved in with Gran after my parents' death, Michael has called me sis. He said he always wanted a little girl, and since Jennifer was unable to have anymore kids, I would do just fine.

Before I can answer Gran speaks up, "Yes, we were just discussing that. Allison has those two bags by the door, which still need to be loaded, and then she's all set."

"Perfect. Sweetheart, I hope you don't mind delivering some goodies to that son of mine. I made a care package for each of you. Cookies, fudge, toiletries, and a few gift cards, among other things," Jennifer tells me.

"Are you kidding? Seeing Ace is my only motivation for even leaving. I hate that I'm leaving Gran alone at night." I give Gran a pleading look that doesn't seem to faze her. "Thank you for the goodies, you really are too good to me," I tell her, wrapping my arms around her for a hug.

"We love you, Allison, you're a part of our family and always will be," she replies softly. "Michael and I will finish loading your car while you say your goodbyes. Are you sure you don't want us to come with you and help you get settled in?"

"No. Thank you, though. I don't really have all that much, and the dorms have elevators, so I won't have to worry about stairs. I've been in contact with my roommate. Her name is Hailey. She's getting there this afternoon as well, so we plan on doing it together." I shrug. "She thought it would help us bond. We met a few weeks ago for pizza, just to get more acquainted." Luckily we live less than an hour drive of each other so we were able to meet up easily.

"I think I like this Hailey character." Gran grins at me.

I lean down to embrace her in a hug, feeling her fragile body in my arms as she whispers, "Life is a giant canvas, Allie, you should throw as much paint on it as you can. You determine your future. I'm so proud of the woman you've become, and your parents would be too."

I pull away from her, tears running down my face. "I love you, Gran. I'll call every day, and, please, call me if you need me. I'm just forty minutes away." I kiss her on the cheek. "I miss you already."

"I miss you too, sweet girl."

The drive to UNC is short and sweet. Thankfully, I'm able to get my emotions under control during the drive. When I reach the parking lot for my dorm, I send Hailey, my roommate, a text.

ME: Hey! Just pulled into the lot.

. . .

HAILEY: Be there in 3 min.

ME: K

TRUE TO HER WORD, Hailey arrives three minutes later, pulling up beside me in her blue Ford Fusion. We've been emailing for two months now, so I feel like I already know her. I don't have a lot of friends. Really, Ace is the only friend I'm close to. I didn't have a lot of time for friendships and hanging out while I was taking care of Gran. My heart squeezes in my chest. I miss her already. As I climb out of the car, Hailey's already heading toward me.

"Allison! I'm so excited!" Hailey screeches as she throws her arms around me for a hug.

Her enthusiasm is infectious. "Me too." I laugh.

"Let's get started. I know we said we were going to do this on our own, but my dad insisted my brother help. He's a senior here at UNC; he and his best friend, Dash, live off campus. Wait, I've told you that already. There he is now." I don't think she even took a breath.

I laugh to myself, what kind of name is Dash? Of course, I'm okay with some muscles to help with the heavy lifting. I assume Hailey's brother is muscular, since he's the quarterback for UNC. The good thing about Hailey and me reaching out to each other the past couple of months is I feel like I already know so much about her. It takes away that awkward feeling of living with a stranger. I've heard a lot about her family, and she knows all about Gran and Ace, of course.

"Allison, did you hear me?" Hailey asks.

I turn to face her... *Holy shit!* Standing next to Hailey is the sexiest guy I've ever seen in my entire life. He's tall, at least six-four, and strong, broad shoulders. His hair is lighter than Hailey's, cut short, and the most staggering sky-blue eyes I've ever seen. I know I'm staring, but I can't seem to control myself. He's wearing blue jeans that hang just right and a plain white t-shirt, which embraces his ripped abs and shoulders.

"Allison, this is my brother. Liam. Liam, this is Allison, my roommate."

Mr. Sexy, also known as Liam, smiles and reaches his hand out to me. "Nice to meet you," he says as he flashes me a charming smile.

I realize I'm still staring, and he's waiting for me to shake his hand. So, I reach out accepting the handshake. "You as well, thanks for your help." There, that sounds normal, a little breathy, but who can blame me. This guy is sex on a stick.

I hear someone clearing their throat. I pull my eyes away from Mr. Sexy and notice there's a huge guy standing right beside him. "This is Blitzen, a friend of mine," Liam tells me.

"Hello, Blitzen, I'm Allison. It's nice to meet you." I study him, partly to keep my eyes from searching for Liam and partly because, well, he's fine. Maybe living in the dorms won't be so bad after all.

Blitzen is close to the same height as Liam, probably six-three, with shaggy, curly, blonde hair. He's built, his blue t-shirt clinging to his muscles. The sleeves on his shirt look like they could rip any minute. His abs are rock hard. I know this because his shirt is skin tight, leaving nothing to the imagination. *No fat on these fellas.*

"The pleasure is all mine, beautiful," Blitzen croons as he leans in and kisses me on the cheek.

Liam reaches out and smacks Blitzen on the back of the head. "Come on, Romeo. Let's get this show on the road."

Blitzen winks at me as we all begin carrying everything up to our dorm room. I have to admit, with the use of two football players at our disposal the move went much faster than if it would have if it had been just Hailey and me. Ace is gonna be pissed when he finds out. He wanted to help and I told him no. Hailey and I wanted to do this together. Her dad shot that plan to hell, but I'm not complaining. Once both cars are unloaded, the guys throw themselves on a futon in our room while digging water out of a cooler I'd packed for the trip. I am nervous being close to two hot guys in such a confined space. The only guy I've really spent any time around was Ace, and we've been friends since I was ten. There were no dates for me in high school, so this is a new experience. I decide I need to break the tension.

"So, Blitzen, that's an interesting name," I say casually.

Blitzen throws his head back and roars with laughter. "That it is, sweetheart, but my real name is Preston. Blitzen is my nickname. I'm a defensive lineman and blitzing is kind of my thing." He shrugs his shoulders. "So, my teammates started calling me that freshman year and it just kind of stuck." He laughs.

"Yeah, Blitzen, Liam, and Dash, Liam's roommate, are all seniors this year and are all in line for the next year's NFL Draft," Hailey gushes.

"Wow. That's awesome. Congrats to both of you," I say, smiling at Blitzen, trying to avoid looking at Liam. I'm afraid of embarrassing myself by drooling over him.

Liam looks as though he's going to speak when his pinging cell phone interrupts him. "That's Dash, we're supposed to be meeting him at the field to run some plays. He doesn't want to be there late. He's meeting up with an 'old friend' tonight, so he says." You can tell by the tone of his voice he's not believing his friend's excuse.

"Hales, see you later. Allison, it was a pleasure meeting you," Liam says before placing his phone to his ear and answering the call.

Blitzen pulls himself off the futon and waves his goodbye, then just like that they're gone, and I release the breath I was holding. I didn't realize how tense I really was being that close to them. *Get it together*, I chide myself. This is my new life. I'm going to have to get used to hanging out with mixed company. Ugh, now I'm talking like Gran. I miss her, and I worry, but she's right. I need to start living life.

CHAPTER TWO

Liam

I WAS ANNOYED when my dad called and requested I help Hailey and her roommate move into their dorm. Dash, Blitzen, and I had plans to go to the practice field and run a few plays. Blitzen, of course, was game. He's all for checking out the new freshmen and trying to pick out his next fling. I, on the other hand, couldn't care less. All I care about is keeping my grades up and focusing on football. Football is my life. I'm majoring in sports medicine as a backup plan, but I really want my shot at the NFL. All I've ever wanted to do is play football. Don't get me wrong, I date, a man has needs, but I'm not a serial dater like Blitzen. Football is my priority, football is my life, and nothing will ever change that. I scratch the itch when I need to, help take the edge off, but nothing more. I don't want or need the drama that comes with relationships. I have the reputation on campus as a player. I don't care what other people think of me, well, unless it's a scout.

"Fuck me, is that Hailey's roommate? She is smokin'," Blitzen says as we climb out of my Pathfinder.

I turn my head to look and standing with my baby sister smiling and laughing is the most striking female I've ever seen. She has long, brown hair that just makes you want to reach out and touch it just to see if it's as soft as it looks. She's a little shorter than Hales, probably five-four with a body that would make any man drool. Now, I'm usually not one to lust after women. Usually, I am the one lusted after. Being the quarterback of the undefeated UNC for the past two years basically puts a target on my back. I don't even have to pretend to be interested to have my needs met. Don't get me wrong, all the girls I'm with know the score. I don't do permanent. It's hard for me to distinguish between who's in it for me and who's in it for my potential NFL future. No commitments on my end. I make sure they enjoy themselves as much as I do, and then we go our separate ways. Football and my dreams of the NFL are my main priority, my life. However, as I stare at this girl laughing with my little sister, I'm overwhelmed with what I can only describe as need ... she's beautiful.

I make my way toward them and stop beside Hales, never taking my eyes off of the beautiful girl in front of me. Hailey bumps my shoulder with hers as she introduces us.

"Allison, this is my brother, Liam. Liam, this is Allison, my roommate."

When she finally looks up at me, I'm mesmerized by her emerald eyes.

"Nice to meet you," I say as I thrust my hand toward her. I smile at her; she seems nervous, not as carefree as she was when we first pulled into the lot. After a few moments she takes my hand.

"You as well, thanks for your help," she says while quickly releasing my hand. *Fuck, her eyes are amazing.* Our gazes remain locked until I hear Blitzen beside me clearing his throat. Reluctantly, I turn to face him.

"This is Blitzen, a friend of mine," I say to Allison. This gives me the chance to look at her without feeling like a damn stalker.

Allison greets Blitzen with a warm smile. "Hello, Blitzen, I'm Allison. It's nice to meet you."

Of course, my horn dog friend is also obviously in lust with this girl; however, he doesn't care to hide it. "The pleasure is all mine, beautiful," he says to Allison as he bends down and kisses her on the cheek. *What the fuck?*

Without even thinking, I smack him on the back of the head. If anyone is calling dibs, it's going to be me.

Watching another man, even one of my closest friends, touch her or kiss her throws me off kilter. If I didn't know any better, I would say I was feeling jealous. But that's not possible. I don't do jealousy. *I need to get laid.*

Blitzen and I proceed to help the girls haul everything up to their dorm room. It takes us all of twenty minutes, and most of that time we were carrying Hailey's things. Allison packed light. When I ask her about it, she just shrugs her shoulders. "I'm only forty minutes from home and plan to visit often," she says as she continues to hang her clothes in her closet.

I'm taken aback by her answer. I have yet to encounter a girl, including my baby sister, who doesn't care about the right clothes, shoes, and a whole other laundry list of accessories they can't seem to live without. Just something else that adds to her appeal. Shaking out of my thoughts I plop down on the futon, Blitzen taking the seat next to me.

We're both quiet as we watch the girls work, well, Allison work, when I get a text from Dash. He's wondering where in the hell we are. I had told him we would be there in thirty minutes tops. That was an hour and a half ago. We stopped and got some lunch before coming here and well, we could have left a half hour ago, but the scenery was too good to pass up. Quickly, we say goodbye, and head to the field.

By the time we get there, Dash is raring to go. He's pissed that we're late, because he's meeting with his best friend, Ash, later tonight. She's a freshman this year at UNC and is arriving today.

Dash insists they're just friends and have been since he was thirteen and she was ten. He talks about her all the time, so, of course, we razz him about it being more. Honestly, either way it's none of my business, but my boy thinks a lot of her. He warned us all last weekend to control ourselves and I quote, '*your horn dog ways around Ash, she's different. Special*'. Just friends my ass. I have yet to see a male and a female in a non-romantic relationship just being friends. I'm not saying that it's impossible, but I've just never been witness to it before. Although he does date and Dash isn't the type of guy to cheat, he's better than that. So, maybe there is something to this just friends business. She's here now, at the same college, living on campus so the truth is bound to come out.

CHAPTER THREE

Allison

HAILEY AND I FINISHED UNPACKING, and now we're lying on our beds relaxing. We were fortunate to have a rather large dorm room with our own private bath and mini kitchenette. We easily unpacked all of our stuff in the shared space. She and I are both fairly laid back and haven't had any issues agreeing yet. We've already discussed our class schedules, so we aren't both trying to use the bathroom at the same time. Classes start on Monday, and we're all set. College life, here we come.

"So," Hailey says as she sits up on her bed, "you think my brother's hot?"

"What? I—um, well, yeah, he's nice to look at, but so is Blitzen," I respond honestly. No sense in trying to deny it, she obviously saw me ogling them earlier today. "Can you honestly blame me? Two beefy, sexy as hell football players with bulging muscles helping us move. Hello, I'm only human."

Hailey busts out in laughter. "First of all, EWWW! This is my big brother we're talking about. Second of all, forsaking the blood-lines, hell yeah, they're both hot. Just wait until you see Dash, he's just as gorgeous, more so than the other two, in my opinion."

"Do I sense a small crush, Hales?"

"Just stating the facts," she says, not committing to the conversation. I can tell she's holding back. "So, what are your plans for tonight?"

"I'm meeting up with Ace. I'm supposed to meet him at Long-horn for dinner at seven. How about you, any plans?"

"I actually have a date with this guy Todd, who graduated with my brother. Todd's a senior at Duke. Please, don't tell Liam, he and Todd don't exactly see eye-to-eye. Liam would flip his lid if he knew I was going out with Todd."

"So, why go?" I ask, intrigued as to why the drama of the situation would be worth it.

Hailey shrugs. "It's just a date, and it's not like we're getting married. Besides, I'm getting the full college experience and dating is a huge part of that." She laughs.

"Well, alright then. Mums the word. Don't tell Liam about Todd, got it."

My cell beeps, alerting me of a new message.

ACE: Hey, are we still on for 7?

ME: Yes. Can't wait 2 c u.

ACE: me 2 cu soon.

"WAS THAT ACE?" Hailey asks me.

"Yeah, he was just making sure we were still on for tonight."

"When am I going to get to meet this guy? Your best friend?" she questions. I can tell from her tone that she's not fully convinced Ace is just my best friend.

"How about we make plans to all get together tomorrow night?" Seeing us together is the only way to prove it. He really is like a big brother to me.

"Sounds like a plan."

An hour later I'm pulling into Longhorn, and I spot Ace immediately. He's standing out front, leaning up against the wall with one foot propped against it. His shaggy brown hair is hanging down over his eyes. He's messing with his phone. As I approach him, he looks up and greets me with a warm smile. I run to him and wrap him in tight hug. "I missed you, Ace," I whisper in his ear.

Ace pulls me tight and kisses the top of my head. "I missed you too, Ash, it's so good to see you."

We proceed to walk into the restaurant and are immediately seated. Ace arrived early to put our name on the list. "So, how's the roommate, Hailey, right?"

I smile. "Yes, Hailey, and she's great. Her brother and his buddy actually helped us move in, which was a huge time saver." I pause, wondering if I should mention how taken I was with Hailey's brother. Ace is my best friend, we talk about everything. However, I've never dated or really been interested in a guy before, so this is new territory for me. Sure, I've talked about actors, bands, or celebrities I thought were hot, but it's never been anyone within reach. Who am I kidding? Liam's out of reach too. *Just spit it out.* "It didn't hurt that he and his friend are hot," I add as I fumble with my napkin.

Ace smiles. "So, you think her brother's hot, huh?"

"Yep." I shrug as if I haven't been thinking about him all afternoon. "Hot and so out of my league, but good eye candy."

"Out of your league? You're kidding me, right? You know you're gorgeous."

"Psh, you're required to say things like that. It's part of your job description as my best friend."

"Ash, listen to me, you are amazing, and I'm sure, whoever this guy is, he's not good enough for you. I don't want to hear anymore of this out of your league shit. Got it?"

I nod my head yes, afraid to let the emotion in my voice show. He's always been there to support me since the day we met. I truly don't know what I would do without him in my life.

"I talked to my parents earlier, they were worried about you. You apparently didn't call and let them know you had arrived."

Shit. "No, I forgot. I did call Gran and let her know, though." I take a sip of my water. "Speaking of your parents, I have a care package for you in my car from your mom." I grin at him, and then stick out my tongue. "She made me one too."

Ace laughs. "Did you expect anything less?" We order our food and get caught up with life in general. It's so good to see him. He had to come back to campus early for football, so I didn't get to see him much this summer.

The waiter brings our food, and we talk while we eat. I tell Ace about Hailey, how much we have in common, how nice it is to have a girl for a friend. He fakes being hurt by this, but I know he understands where I'm coming from. He talks about football and how excited he is that his team has gone undefeated the last two years. He talks about his hopes to carry that on this year, being it's his last year at UNC and on the football field. Unless the draft comes through for him, that is. If not, he'll be a free agent, which makes his chances slim for getting picked up by any of the NFL teams. He always has his degree of Sports Medicine to fall back on.

I want to tell Ace that Hailey's sexy as sin brother is on his team as well, but decide against it. I know Ace would know him, and I don't want to deal with the teasing and the lecture that will follow my admission.

As we finish our dessert, a hot fudge sundae we split, I remember I'd promised Hailey we would all go out tomorrow night. "Hey, do you have plans tomorrow night?" I ask Ace.

"Nope."

"Great, Hailey wants to meet you. I've talked about you so much she wants to see if you live up to all the hype," I tease.

Ace chuckles. "I'm down, I'll see if Mac wants to go as well."

"Awesome sauce, we both get to meet each other's roommates tomorrow night. Where should we go?"

"Let's meet up at The Warehouse. A guy on the team's dad owns it, so we get VIP treatment." He winks at me. "Meet you guys there at eight?"

I nod in agreement.

We argue over who is going to pay for dinner, I lose the battle. After paying he follows me out to my car, so I can give him his care package from his mom. With a farewell hug, we go our separate ways.

When I arrive back at the dorm, Hailey is fully engrossed in her Kindle, yet another thing we have in common. I fill her in on the plans for tomorrow night before taking a fast shower, making quick calls to the Emersons and Gran, before going to bed. It's been a long and exhausting day.

As I climb into bed, Hailey informs me that tomorrow night is country night at The Warehouse, and she and I are hitting the mall tomorrow to ensure we're dressed appropriately. I fall asleep with a smile on my face. I'm getting to live the normal life my peers have been living. I miss Gran, but I love her for pushing me to do this. Not bad for a first day.

CHAPTER FOUR

Liam

AFTER DROPPING Blitzen off at his place, I decide to hit the gym. I'd already been there first thing this morning, but I need a distraction. All day long I've been thinking about Allison. The way I can't get her out of my mind is like nothing I've ever experienced. I can't wrap my head around it. I've only spent two hours with her and she's consuming my thoughts. I work out for a couple of hours, hit the showers, and head home. There's no way in hell I can act on this... attraction I'm feeling for her. She's my sister's roommate. Hailey would kill me.

I pull into the lot of our complex at the same time as Aiden, also known as Dash, my roommate does. Dash is our running back and 'speed' is his thing, hence the nickname. "Hey, man! I thought you were meeting up with Ash tonight?"

"I did, we had dinner at Longhorn. She gave me this," he says, smiling as he lifts a large basket filled with goodies. It looks just like

the one that Allison brought up to her room earlier today. *There I go
again.*

"Is that from your mom?" I ask. My mouth is already watering.
Aiden's mom is an amazing cook and always sends the best treats.

"Why yes it is. Can I possibly interest you in banana bread, buck-
eyes, or a peanut butter cookie, perhaps?"

"Dude, stop teasing and share the love," I whine. "I'm starving, I
haven't had dinner yet."

"You should've come with me, you could've met Ash."

I raise my eyebrows at him. "I wouldn't intrude on your date,
man, not cool."

"How many times do I have to tell you? It's not like that with
Ash. She's like my little sister. Her parents died in a car crash when
she was ten. She came to live with her gran, who lives next door to my
parents. She was shy and scared, and my parents fell in love with her
immediately. It's really kind of hard not to. Anyway, they asked me to
take her under my wing, look out for her at school and things. She
became my best friend. I love her like my little sister. I've never had
romantic feelings for her."

"You just said it's hard to not fall in love with her," I remind him.

"Yes, it is, and when you meet her, you'll know why. There are
many different types of love. She's family, that's all."

"Okay, I hear what you're saying, but you warned all of us off of
her like she was yours, man."

"That's because, she's different." He runs his hands through his hair,
obviously struggling with something. "Listen, man, I don't want the
other guys to know this. You're my best friend, other than Ash, so I know
I can trust you. I don't want those other vultures to get wind of this." He
takes a deep breath. "Ash is innocent, man. She's never been on a date,
she's never even been kissed. Her parents were both college professors,
so she spent all of her time studying and making grades. It was her way of
honoring their memory and making them proud. Any spare time she
had, she was taking care of her gran. Gran is old and her health is failing

fast. Ash took care of her. They took care of each other. Granny Hagan is her only family. My parents and I adopted them into ours. My dad calls her sis, and we're all she'll have left when something happens to Gran."

We sit in silence for a few minutes. "Wow, she has no other family?"

"Nope, both of her parents were only children, and her mom's parents both passed on before she was born. It's just her and Gran."

"Damn." I'm trying to process all that I've just learned.

"She's amazing, the strongest person I know. She's not like the girls we're used to; she doesn't bitch and whine all the time. She's been dealt a bad hand in life, but she keeps her head up and just lives for each day. She constantly worries and fusses over her gran, but it's endearing. Her gran had to make her stay on campus. She wanted to drive back and forth each day, just so she would be there if her gran needed her. It took a lot of convincing from my parents and Gran's home-care nurse that Gran would be well cared for to get her to go through with it." He takes a deep breath and runs his hands through his hair again. "She didn't go to prom. I told her that I would come home and take her, she refused. Said she didn't need her best friend to be her pity date. The thing is, she had offers, tons of them, she's beautiful, but she always turned them down. Gran came first. Instead, she stayed in, and she and Gran watched movies and ate popcorn. So, you see, Ash is different, special. Once the guys get wind of all of this, her innocence, it'd become a challenge for them. I want better for her, more. She deserves better, she deserves respect and love. She needs to find someone who'll make her the center of their universe, because that's what they would be for her." He rests his head against the back of the couch.

Fuck! Now I feel bad for always razzing him. "I see, now, where you're coming from. I get it." I get up to get more cookies out of the basket. *Damn things are addicting.* "So, I helped Hales move into her dorm today." I need to change the subject.

"Oh, yeah, so your little sis is officially a college student."

"Yep, she's really excited, her roommate was there, she's...beauti-ful." *What the hell, did I just say that?*

Aiden throws his head back and laughs. "Wow, that's huge coming from you. You feeling alright?"

It's my turn to run my hand through my hair, trying to process what I want to say. "Fuck if I know. This girl has consumed my thoughts all damn day. I spent two hours with her and Hales, and now she's all that I can think about. I can't describe it, there's just something about her. She's gorgeous and I'm drawn to her, man. I know this sounds fucked up, and I'm in major jeopardy of losing my man card, but I can't seem to stop thinking about her."

I plop down beside him on the couch with the entire cookie container. "Get this shit. I shook her hand when Hales introduced us and when she let go it bothered me. What the fuck is that about? I'd just met this girl, and I didn't want her to let go of my hand." I take a drink of milk. "Go ahead and say it, I'm a pussy." I take another drink of milk. "Then, when I introduced Blitzen, he kissed her cheek, and I wanted to punch him. So, tell me what the fuck is going on with me?"

Aiden chuckles. "Sounds to me like it's love at first sight." He winks at me, winding me up even further.

I take a minute to process what he said, and to finish the cookie I just shoved into my mouth, *addicting fuckers*. "Do you believe in that shit, love at first sight? I mean, I've heard my dad talk about the moment he met my mother that he knew he wanted to spend the rest of his life with her. I thought he was just spouting shit to me and Hales. Besides, you know me, I don't do relationships. My commit-ment is football."

Aiden doesn't hesitate. "I do, actually. I heard the same story growing up from my parents. More so from my dad, it took Mom a few months to warm up to him." He laughs. "I thought you would flip out on me from my comment, it didn't seem to faze you. You're really into this girl."

"Fuck, man, I don't know. I know I've never had this reaction to anyone before in my life, maybe I just need to get laid," I say, repeating my thoughts from earlier today.

"All I can say is when I find someone who makes me think of them all day long after only being in their presence for two hours, I'll pursue it and see where it goes." He shrugs as though the decision should be obvious.

"She's Hailey's roommate. I don't want to cause problems with them. Football and the draft, that's what I have to focus on. If I hooked up with her, it'd be awkward seeing her all the time. She and my sister hung out over the past couple of months and kept in touch. Hales really likes her. I can't do that to my sister."

"Well, maybe this girl will be *the one*. Are you going to risk letting *the one* go?" he says, smirking. He's getting some form of satisfaction watching me squirm.

"Alright, that's enough girl talk for one night, my head is spinning," I declare. I have to get this chick out of my head. She's beautiful, yes, and I'm insanely attracted to her. I'll go out tomorrow night, hookup, and get this out of my system. This has just been an off day.

Aiden laughs. "Hey, Ash and I are going to The Warehouse tomorrow night. She's bringing her roommate, so I can meet her. You should come with us, maybe it'll help get your mind off of Hailey's roommate. Besides, Ash mentioned she met her roommate's brother and thought he was hot. You can meet her and see if you know the guy, see if I have to warn him off."

"I'm in." I don't even hesitate. The Warehouse is a local hangout and the perfect environment to let go and clear my thoughts of Allison.

CHAPTER FIVE

Allison

HAILEY and I sleep in our first morning in the dorm, which is new for me. I'm usually up at the break of dawn with Gran, making sure she has her meds and breakfast. We shower and decide to grab a bagel at Starbucks on our way to the mall. Last night as I lay in bed, I decided I was going to embrace college life. Like Gran had said, I need to pave my way. I know she's thinking about when she's no longer here with me. Her health is failing, and just the thought of losing her brings tears to my eyes. I'm going to make Gran proud of me, starting today. I'm going to re-vamp my wardrobe, act and dress my age. Money isn't an issue for me. My parents were older and well established in their careers when they had me. They had planned well for their futures and mine. I received a trust on my eighteenth birthday last September. I have more than enough money to never have to work. I could easily live on my monthly allowance from the interest alone. I could, but I don't want to. I'm excited to be going to college and experiencing life like kids my age.

"Okay, so tonight is country night at The Warehouse, we need to embrace that," Hailey says as we walk into the mall. Apparently, The Warehouse has themes they rotate through to keep a broad range of customers coming through their doors.

"Sounds good to me, I'm actually thinking I need to upgrade my wardrobe. I didn't ever go out back home. I was always taking care of Gran or worrying about school. I think I'm past due for a makeover."

Hailey's eyes sparkle. "EEEK! I'm so excited! Let's work on tonight's wardrobe first, so we know we're covered, and then go from there."

I laugh at her excitement. "Let's do this thing," I say, looping my arm through hers as we make our way in to the Gap. This is where I find the perfect blue jean skirt for tonight. I also purchase jeans, tank tops, sweaters, and shorts.

We spend the entire day at the mall, making multiple trips to my car to unload our loot. We go to Victoria's Secret last and spend way too much money on sexy underwear and bras I never would have thought I'd be wearing. Hailey assures me these items are essential, even if no one ever sees them. "They help make you feel sexy," she tells me. I'm still unsure, but I trust her judgment, besides this is all new to me. What do I know? All my underwear came from Walmart. I also purchase all new makeup, get my hair cut, so does Hailey. We both get a manicure and a pedicure. I feel like I've been overhauled, but I'm excited, I cannot remember the last time I had this much fun.

It takes us three trips to carry everything up to our dorm room. *Yes, we went overboard.* We dump all of our purchases out on our beds. I ended up with four pairs of jeans, fifteen shirts or tanks, four sweaters, two pair of shorts, a skirt, a pair of ballet flats, two pair of flip-flops, a pair of Puma tennis shoes, and a pair of cowboy boots. Hailey had insisted that we needed them to complete our outfits for tonight. Add in the sexy new bras, panties, haircut, and the mani-pedi, and I'm a new woman. Hailey bought almost as much as I did, as I said before, the girl loves her clothes. I asked what her parents were going to say when they saw her credit card bill. She shrugged as if it was no big deal.

"Okay, so I know you originally bought the skirt for tonight, but seeing all this laid out I'm really liking the white shorts," Hailey says as we put our purchases away.

I shrug. "I'm new to all of this. I'm so out of my element. You pick out what you think is best and that's what I'll wear. I trust you." I find myself meaning what I say. Over the summer I'd talked to Hailey a lot on the phone and via the web, and I know she's a good person, she wouldn't steer me wrong.

This makes Hailey very happy. Clapping, she says, "Yeah, okay, so I say you wear the white shorts, the purple and white tanks layered, and the cowboy boots." You can hear the excitement in her voice.

"Are you sure? Those shorts are really short." Hailey had talked me into getting them. She said showing so much leg would drive the guys crazy. I caved and bought them. I know I'm decent looking. I had several offers in school, just no desire. I had Gran to think of and my grades, I wanted to make my parents proud. Now it's time to start living for me, and figuring out who I am. I can still make them proud, but I need to find me in the process.

"Yes, trust me. Now hit the shower, we only have two hours, and we both have to shower and do our makeup." We both had our hair cut and styled, so that was done. Mine was cut into long layers. She styled it by braiding my bangs down the side of my head and pulling all of it in a low side ponytail. It actually looks really good. My thick ponytail hangs down over the front of my shoulder, which exposes the braid on the opposite side. I express my worry it makes me look too young; I still liked it, but I wasn't sure it was fit for a club setting. Hailey assures me that with my outfit it's sexy. *I guess we'll see.*

After we both shower and get dressed, Hailey sets me down on the toilet seat, so she can work her magic on my makeup. "I'm telling you right now, you're going to have every male in The Warehouse falling at your feet tonight. You look hot," she states as she hands me a mirror to view her masterpiece.

I reluctantly take the mirror from her, and I'm struck speechless. Hailey didn't go overboard, she went with subtle light purple eye shadow, mascara, and a light pink lip gloss. *Holy shit!* I stand up and wrap her in a hug. "Thank you," I manage to utter.

"Hey, none of that, or you'll smear my masterpiece. You're beautiful, Allie."

I pull back from her. "I feel beautiful," I whisper.

"It's the undies." She winks at me. "You are beautiful! This is a bonus for me, because I can assure you I won't be buying any drinks tonight with you by my side. Now come on, or we're going to be late. I need to go meet my male counterpart, so hop to it, missy," she scolds me.

We arrive at The Warehouse right at eight o'clock. Ace sent me a text telling me he and his roommate, Mac, were already there. They'd gotten us a booth near the back. Hailey and I make our way toward the back of the club while Florida Georgia Line sings about getting their shine on. Hailey and I are already swaying to the music as we walk.

"Hey, there's my brother. Let's stop and say hi. Do you see Ace anywhere?" Hailey asks me.

I look up and stop dead in my tracks. Liam is sitting in a booth, looking good enough to eat, and beside him...is Ace. *What the hell?* They're deep in conversation, so they don't see us until we step up beside them.

Ace, who's sitting on the outside of the booth, sees me and immediately he stands up and wraps his arms around me, giving me a big hug. "You look amazing," he whispers to me. As he pulls away I can see the questions in Hailey's eyes.

"You know Dash?" she questions me.

"Dash? This is Ace, um well, Aiden, my best friend I was telling you about," I tell her. Aiden releases his hold on me and sits back down beside what appears to be an angry Liam. Hailey motions for me to scoot into the booth, so I do. This left me sitting directly in front of Liam and Hales in front of Aiden.

"So, let me get this straight, Aiden here, also known to us as Dash, is your Ace?" Hailey's trying to untangle the connection.

Aiden laughs.

"Yes, Ace is the name I call him. It's his initials, Aiden Cole Emerson. I've called him that since I first met him," I explain. "To me he's Ace, sometimes Aiden, and to you, well, he's obviously Dash."

My thoughts drift to the day that I first met Aiden:

Sitting on Gran's back porch swing, I scrunch my eyes, trying to keep my tears from falling. Today was the day I had to say my final goodbye to Mommy and Daddy. I've been trying to be really strong and show I can handle it, I don't like for Gran to see me cry. It makes her sad.

Some lady I have never met steps up on the porch. This has happened a lot the last two days. I've met and hugged a lot of strangers. Gran says they worked with my parents.

"You dear child, come give me a hug," she says as she leans down and embraces me. I can feel the burn in my eyes. No matter how hard I squint, I know my tears are going to come.

She turns and heads for the door, mumbling about how I still haven't spoken to anyone. I don't really have anything to say. I'm sad my parents are gone. I wait until she's in the door, before I bolt off the swing and run to my favorite spot, the large oak tree. I reach the tree and slide down the side, bury my face in my knees, and let my tears fall. My only hope is Granny doesn't find me before I can get myself together.

I'm not sure how much time has passed when I hear footsteps in the leaves. I raise my head and see the dark haired boy who was at the funeral. He sits down beside me.

"Hey. My name's Aiden," he says to me. "I live next door, we're going to be neighbors." He's trying to make conversation. I don't want to talk. "What's your name?"

I keep my face buried in my knees and don't respond to him. The next thing I know he's singing. "Aiden, Aiden ,bo-baiden, Banana-fanna-fo-faden, Fee-fi-mo-maiden, Aiden!"

I can't help the giggle that escapes, he's funny. He's also the first person who hasn't mentioned my parents, or how I'm the poor orphan girl. I slightly raise my head to look at him.

"What's your name?" he asks again.

"Allison Shay Hagan," I tell him, and he nods as he starts to sing.

"Allison, Allison, bo-ballison, Banana-fanna-fo-fallison, Fee-fi-mo-mallison, Allison!" he sings.

I lift my head and gift him with a smile, but I don't say anything. This doesn't seem to bother Aiden, he just keeps on talking.

"Allison Shay Hagan, hey, your initials spell ash. I think that'll be my new nickname for you." He bumps my shoulder. "What do you think, Ash?"

"My daddy used to call me princess," I tell him softly. The first words I've spoken, since Gran told me about the accident.

"Well, I like Ash, so that's what I'll call you from now on," he states.

"What's your name, your initials, I mean?" I ask him.

He smiles at me. "Aiden Cole Emerson, Ace."

"Can I call you Ace?"

He's already nodding his head yes. "Yeah, it'll be our thing. You'll be my Ash, and I'll be your Ace."

Hailey's loud laugh brings me back to the conversation. "Wow, what a small world. I guess you never put two and two together did ya, big guy?" Hailey says to Aiden.

"Not in the slightest," Aiden replies, laughing. "Ash, also known as Allison Shay Hagan, this is my roommate Mac, also known as Liam MacCoy, Hailey's older brother." Aiden suddenly whips his head toward Liam and gives him a curious look. Liam just nods his head yes. They must have some kind of super-secret guy language going on.

I'm mortified, not only does Aiden know Liam, but he's his roommate and best friend, other than me of course. I told Aiden last night I thought Hailey's older brother was hot. *Damn*. He's never gonna let me live this down.

CHAPTER SIX

Liam

AIDEN and I arrive at The Warehouse about fifteen minutes to eight. We grab a booth near the back, and Aiden sends Ash a text letting her know where to find us. We chose to sit on the same side of the booth, allowing the girls to sit together to avoid any awkwardness. As we're talking, I look up and spot my sister. Beside her stands Allison, and I just about swallow my fucking tongue. If I thought she was beautiful yesterday, today my brain cannot seem to find the right word to describe her. She's wearing short white shorts, showing off her amazing legs, a purple and white tank top, and her hair is pulled to the side exposing one side of her neck. *All that skin.* My eyes travel back down to her legs and that's when I notice the black cowboy boots, *fuck me that's hot!* I'm so engrossed in Allison I don't even realize she and Hales have stopped at our table. I'm brought out of my trance when Aiden stands up and wraps his arms around her. *What the fuck!* Why is he hugging her? I've never in my life been so happy to hear my little sister's voice as she questions them.

I sit quietly, listening to their explanation. Apparently, my Allison is also Aiden's Ash. *Well, fuck me!* My thoughts immediately go to my conversation last night with Aiden at the same time his must have done the same. He turns to look at me as if to tell me if I hurt her, I'm a dead man. I simply nod my head. I understand. He also needs to understand that even with the recent turn of events, my attraction to her hasn't wavered. *I am so screwed.* So much for using tonight to work her out my system. *Fuck!*

"Well, now that we have that all sorted out, let's get us some drinks." Hailey smiles sweetly at me. She's only eighteen, so I'll have to buy them for her. She's been to a couple of our parties, and I let her drink, but she had to stay there with me. Before I can respond to Hailey, Aiden is talking to Allison.

"Ash, have you eaten anything?" he asks, concerned

"Yes, Hailey and I went to the deli on campus on our way here," Allison tells him.

I'm a little slow on the uptake. "Wait, Allison, have you ever drank before?" I ask her, concern lacing my voice.

She blushes, and I think even that's sexy on her. "No," she whispers quietly.

Her soft sultry voice is going to put me over the edge. I look at Hales. "Maybe you guys should take it easy tonight." What I really want to say is I don't want either of them drinking at all tonight. Not looking like they do in a bar full of horny, drunk college guys. I would hate to have to throw any punches; coach would be on my ass. I have to look after Hales, she's my baby sister. Now, I also feel this protective pull toward Allison. These feelings are pissing me off, and I can feel my anger increasing at just the thought of someone touching either one of them.

"Ash, maybe Liam is right. You should take it slow tonight, considering the crowd." He peers around the room, obviously thinking the same thing I am.

"Fine," she grumbles. "But what happened to living the full college experience?"

Aiden chuckles. "I promise we'll have you living the full college experience, you won't get short changed. Let's just take it slow for tonight, alright?" He smirks at her.

"Okay, okay, start her off on something mild, like a weak daiquiri. I, on the other hand, big brother, would like a shot of tequila to start off my night." Hailey winks at me.

Aiden and I go to the bar and order drinks for the girls. Aiden gets a Corona for himself, and I pass on a beer, just ordering Mountain Dew. "What's up?" he asks me.

I place my hands on the back of my neck and just look at him and shake my head before blurting it out. "One of us needs to stay sober to keep an eye on them." I know I'm over reacting, but I can't get the image of some douchebag all over them out of my head.

Aiden looks confused. "Hales has been drinking plenty of times, she can handle herself, and I'll keep a close eye on Allison. You might as well have a drink, man. We don't have to get trashed."

I'm shaking my head no before he's even finished. "Not happening," I grumble. If I'm going to keep a close eye on both of them, I need a clear head.

Aiden stares at me in disbelief. "Liam," he says in warning. He knows me so well. He can tell I'm a fucking wreck over this girl.

"Look, man, I can't explain this. I wouldn't even know where to start. I feel this connection to her, this need to protect her, just like I would Hales." I run my hands through my hair. "No, not just like Hales—fuck! I would lay my life down for my little sister, but this feeling I have for Allison, well, it's not exactly brotherly," I admit.

"She's my sister in every sense of the word. Don't hurt her, Liam, or I swear to God." He takes a deep breath. "She's not just a quick fuck that you don't ever speak to again. So help me, if you hurt her in any way, I will beat the shit out of you. She's *my* baby sister. FUCK!" He's now just as frustrated as I am. I get it, but I still can't help it.

I hold up my hands to stop him. "I. will. Not. Hurt. Her. I promise you, man. This isn't a game to me. I heard everything you said last night, but you heard me as well. I didn't even know my

Allison was your Ash last night, and I opened up to you about her. Trust me," I plead with him.

Aiden looks at me with a raised eyebrow. "You said my Allison."

What the fuck? "I did not." Damn, this girl has got me tied in knots.

Aiden slaps me on the back. "You're my best friend, but I won't hesitate to choose Ash over you. She's my sister for all intents and purposes. Think about Hales and what you would do if one of the guys used her, hurt her." He steps back from me. "Don't fuck with her, Liam. I mean it."

With that being said, we walk back to the booth and deliver the drinks to the girls. Hales questions my lack of alcohol, and I just play it off that someone needs to be the designated driver. It was a likely excuse. The way my head is spinning, I need to stay sober anyway.

Hailey slams her shot as Allison chugs her daiquiri. Good thing Aiden had them weaken it for her. *Thank you, Aiden!* Hailey jumps up and pulls Allison out on the dance floor. *Fuck, here we go.* Allison is a sex goddess, and my sister is just as beautiful, wearing clothes that show way too much skin. I can't help but notice how even Aiden is checking her out. I should give him the same speech he just gave me.

My eyes never leave the girls on the dance floor. They are currently grinding to "Save a Horse Ride a Cowboy". The song has just started when I see two drunk fuckers come up to each of them, putting their hands all over them. My blood starts to boil. Aiden slides out of the booth and I follow him. I look over at him and motion toward Hailey, he nods that he understands. We stalk toward the dance floor, to the girls, with purpose.

Aiden walks up to Hales, stands in front of her, and pulls her to him. The guy behind her, grinding up on her, immediately backs off when Aiden gives him a warning look. It helps that Hales screeches Aiden's name as she throws her arms around his neck.

The dickwad that's all over Allison is at her front, and I can tell by her posture she's very uncomfortable. I walk up behind her and put my hands on her waist, pulling her back against my chest. I lean down and kiss her exposed neck. "Work with me, sweetheart, so we can get rid of your friend," I whisper in her ear.

Allison simply nods her head and pushes her body back into mine. I too have to impose a threatening glare, and it works. Dickwad throws his hands up and stalks off. I sigh with relief that she's in my arms. It's then I realize she's still dancing and swaying to the music. Hales has turned to place her back to Aiden's front, as well, and we're all laughing and having a good time. The song changes to Colt Ford's "Dancing While Intoxicated", and I smile. Allison isn't pulling away, so I decide to embrace it and hold her close.

Hailey and Aiden are getting pretty cozy; she reaches up and wraps her arms around his neck still grinding in front of him. She winks at Allison, who seems to take that as her cue to mimic them. Allison reaches up and places her hands behind my neck, and as she does I lean down and put my face in the crook of her neck, breathing her in. Her hair being pulled to one side is sexy as hell, and turning out to be quite a convenience for me. She turns her head to look at me and gives me a shy smile. We continue to bump and grind to the beat of the music, and I'm lost in her.

As the music turns slower to "You Won't Ever Be Lonely", Allison starts to pull away. I seize the opportunity to turn her toward me and hold her tight. "Dance with me, sweetheart," I whisper in her ear. I can see Aiden watching us as he pulls Hailey closer. I don't care, besides he's nuzzled up with *my* sister. If this is as close as I can get to her, I'm going to take full advantage. I know what Aiden said is right; I'm not that guy, the one looking to settle down with one girl. Allison deserves her happily ever after, the kind a guy like me can't give her.

Her only reply is to wrap her arms around my waist and lay her head on my chest. She's so tiny and fits perfectly in my arms. I sigh deeply; I'm so relaxed in this moment. I pull her tighter and began to sing softly to her.

Before I even realize it, the song is over and another slow one begins. Allison makes no move to pull away. At this moment, it would take a small army to pull me away from her, as Kenny Chesney sings about having him from hello. I smile and think to myself, *she most certainly did.*

Allison adjusts her hold on me and wraps her arms all the way around my waist. I feel something move inside of me. I don't even know how to express these feelings I'm experiencing. Something tells me she's feeling it too, but I know too much about her. I can't give her what she wants, what she deserves. I place a soft kiss on the top of her head and close my eyes, enjoying the feel of her in my arms while it lasts.

The song ends, and I think I hear Hailey telling Aiden to buy her another drink. Allison raises her head from my chest and looks up at me. I place my forehead against hers. I want to kiss her so damn bad, but I don't want her first kiss to be here in a smoky bar surrounded by drunks, it needs to be special. I lock my gaze on her emerald green eyes and emotion swarms me. I have to swallow the lump in my throat before saying, "Thank you for the dance, sweetheart," and kissing her on the forehead. I link her fingers through mine and guide her to the booth, where Aiden and Hailey already have fresh drinks waiting.

CHAPTER SEVEN

Allison

"I CAN'T BELIEVE that your Ace is our Aiden. What a small world," Hailey says to me. Aiden and Liam are at the bar getting our drinks.

I simply nod my head, I'm still trying to wrap my head around the fact I'd told Aiden I thought my roommate's brother, who also happens to be his roommate, is hot! I hope he keeps his mouth shut.

"Here we go, ladies," Aiden says as he places our drinks in front of us.

"Where's yours?" Hailey asks Liam.

"One of us needs to be the designated driver." Liam shrugs his shoulders.

Hot isn't really an accurate description of Liam. He's tall with broad shoulders and defined muscles. The faded blue jeans and black dress shirt he's wearing with the sleeves rolled up to his forearms shows off his body perfectly. As usual, when I am in his presence, I need a distraction, so what do I do? I chug my strawberry daiquiri.

I'm sure Aiden had them make it weak. However, when chugging, I can still feel the effects.

Hailey grabs me by the arm and pulls me out of the booth. "Come on, roomie, let's get our dance on."

I laugh as I let her pull me to the dance floor. Big and Rich are singing about saving a horse and riding a cowboy. I try to clear my thoughts of Liam and just feel the music. I've never been dancing. My only slow dances have been with Aiden and his father at their family functions Gran and I would attend if she was feeling up to it. Gran and I would dance around the house. There were many times Aiden would catch us and join in the fun. That about sums up my limited experience. I have my eyes closed, feeling the music when I feel strong hands grab my hips. I open my eyes to see a blond-haired guy about six foot, maybe. He's built, but Aiden and Liam both put him to shame. He's obviously drunk and keeps trying to pull me to him. I place my hands on his chest to push him away, but he's not taking no for an answer. I'm starting to panic, I've never been in this type of situation before.

Suddenly, I feel warmth on my back, and strong arms come around me at the same time I see Aiden come up behind Hales. I glance over to see Liam's striking blue gaze. He leans down and kisses my neck while whispering in my ear, "Work with me, sweetheart, so we can get rid of your friend." I nod my acceptance. That is all that I can do. The warmth of him wrapped around me and the feel of his kiss on my neck mix with his soft words in my ear. *I'm a flippin' mess!* Butterflies take over my stomach. Speech isn't something I'm currently capable of. Mr. Drunk and Grabby takes the hint and backs away.

I continue swaying my hips, and Liam pulls me closer to him. The song changes to "Dancing While Intoxicated", and I smile. *I most certainly am, or starting to be.* I know I've only had one drink, but chugging my first alcoholic beverage wasn't the best choice on my part. I'm feeling pretty relaxed, otherwise, I would've never had the courage to grind against Liam. Hailey winks at me as she places her hands behind Aiden's neck. I decide to take that as advice and mirror her actions with Liam. I'm nervous as to how he'll react, but I shouldn't have been. He leans down further and places his face in the crook of my neck. He's so close to me, and I can hear him breathing me in. I'm trying not to freak out. Liam is so sexy, and I know he's just being nice to me because of Hailey and Aiden, but for this one moment, I want it to be real. I want him to want me. So, I block out my racing mind and just feel him close to me.

As the music turns slow, I sigh. I know my time with Liam is up, so I release his neck and begin to walk away. Before I can take two steps, Liam has me twirled around and pressed tight against his chest. "Dance with me, sweetheart," he whispers in my ear. I'm still unable to speak for fear this moment isn't real, and I'll wake up from this amazing fantasy to find I'm no longer in his strong arms. I clasp my arms around his waist and lay my head on his chest.

I feel Liam sigh as he pulls me in tighter and begins to softly sing along with the song. My heart feels like it's about to beat out of my chest. Liam holds me like I'm his lifeline, and the words he sings...I know he has no idea about my past, or my fear of always being alone, but in this moment I feel safe and... cherished. I feel the words deep in my soul, as though he's singing them just for me.

The song ends, and I refuse to be the first to let go. I won't let go of him until he pulls away. I feel like the weight of the world has been lifted off my shoulders. I need to feel that a little longer, so I hold him tighter. I feel Liam lean down and kiss the top of my head, then he rests his cheek there. We slowly sway to Kenny Chesney telling us the love of his life had him from hello. *I know the feeling.* Liam's slowly rubbing my back, and I feel my heart shift. In the arms of this man, I can see the future I want, a family, someone to love me. I know it could never be Liam, but I realize that's my dream, I think about Gran and her words to me, *"Life is a giant canvas, Allie, and you should throw as much paint on it as you can."* My dream is to have a family, a husband, kids, in-laws. Yes, in-laws. I'll take all the family I can get, anyway I can get it. It's just been Gran and me for so long now. Aiden's family has adopted me into theirs, and I love them dearly, but I want more. Selfish, I know, but it is what it is.

The music changes again back to a fast tempo, and I lift my head to chance a look into Liam's baby blue eyes. He rests his forehead against mine. "Thank you for the dance, sweetheart," he whispers. I'm worried he can hear the thunderous beat of my heart. He kisses my forehead, laces his fingers through mine, and directs me through the crowd back toward the booth. Hailey and Aiden are there now, sitting beside one another with fresh drinks for all of us. Liam lifts our entwined hands to his lips and kisses the back of my hand, then places his hand on the small of my back and guides me into the booth.

The four of us continue to sit, laughing and talking. Aiden and Liam keep us supplied with drinks. Liam's still sitting next to me with his arm draped over the back of the booth. He's lazily making circles on my shoulder. He's driving me insane. The attraction I feel for him is like nothing I've ever felt. It scares the shit out of me. Liam isn't exactly what you would call a player, but Hailey has told me multiple times he doesn't date and is never serious about anyone. Football is his life. As much as I want the college experience, I also want the love and connection. One-night stands and hookups aren't my thing, and never will be. I want more. Dancing with Liam tonight confirmed that for me. I can never be a hookup for him, and he can never be committed to anyone. I know nothing will go beyond innocent flirting, no matter how sexy he is. I've just confirmed to myself, I'm an all or nothing girl, and I vow to stay true to that.

"I need the ladies' room," Hailey announces. "Allison, come with me?"

I nod my head as Liam and Aiden let us out of the booth. Aiden looks at both of us. "Be careful, if you aren't back in ten minutes, I'm coming to look for you." I try to focus on what he's saying, I really do, but Liam has his hand on the small of my back again as we were waiting for Aiden to finish lecturing us on safety.

Hailey winks at them and pulls me away to the ladies' room. Once inside she smiles at me. "My brother's into you."

I feel my face flush. "He's just being friendly," I manage to reply.

Hailey giggles, we're definitely feeling the drinks. "He's different with you."

I shrug. "Let's do our business and get out of here. I don't want Aiden coming to hunt us down."

As we exit the ladies' room, "Country Girl" by Luke Bryan comes blaring through the sound system, so that's exactly what we do all the way back to the guys. Once we reach our booth, we continue doing what Luke asks us to, and continue our onset of shaking and grooving. I watch as Aiden and Liam stand up from the table. I'm excited thinking they're going to join us on the dance floor. Before I realize what is happening, Aiden has me by the waist and is leading me to the exit. I look back to see Liam following with an angry expression, pulling Hailey with him.

"Hey! We aren't ready to leave," Hailey slurs.

"Too damn bad," Liam growls and pulls her tight against him. "We need to get you two home, so that you can sober up."

Aiden helps me into the passenger seat of my car before turning to Liam. "I'll meet you back at the house. I'm just going to bring Ash with me; I don't want her being alone in case she gets sick."

"Hey, what I am shopped liver?" Hailey slurs.

Aiden laughs. "That's chopped liver, Hales, and no offense, but you're in no shape to take care of anyone."

Aiden helps me into his apartment and leads me to the kitchen table. I plop down in the chair and put my head down. I'm starting to really feel the effects of the alcohol. The excitement of the bar kept me going, but now that things are quiet and calm, I can feel my head pounding.

Aiden touches my shoulder. "Here, Ash, drink this and take these." He hands me a bottle of water and two Advil.

Hailey dumps herself into the chair beside me and groans.

"Here, Hales, take these and drink up." He hands her the same regimen. Apparently, Aiden is trying to prevent us from feeling like a dog's ass the next day, or so I think I hear him say.

"Ash, you need to drink all the water," Aiden scolds me.

"Too tired," I mumble.

Aiden chuckles. "Just drink it all, and then you can sleep, Ash."

I pull my head up from the table to scowl at him, but it hurts too badly to frown. I'm sure whatever expression I'm wearing is rather amusing, considering their smiles. Aiden and Liam are both leaning against the kitchen counter with their legs crossed, smirking at us. *Assholes.*

I'm tired and just want to sleep, so I do as I'm told and finish off the water. I go to stand up and lose my balance. Aiden and Liam both reach for me, but I grab onto Aiden. "Now can I sleep, Ace?" I whisper.

"Yes, you can sleep. Let's get you to bed."

"Shhhh," I whisper, "there's no need to yell."

Aiden just laughs as he leads me down the hall and into his room. I plop down on the bed, and he hands me one of his old football jerseys to sleep in. "Get changed, I'll be right back," he tells me.

CHAPTER EIGHT

Liam

DRUNK ALLISON IS ADORABLE. I stand in the kitchen beside Aiden, waiting for her and Hales to take the Advil and drink the bottle of water Aiden has given them. I glance at my sister. I've seen her in this state before. She usually stays over and either sleeps on the couch or with me, depending on what's going on. Tonight, however, Blitzen is passed out on our couch. Apparently, his roommate is using their place. He texted earlier and asked if it was cool. I mentioned it to Aiden and he was okay with it. Blitzen knew where the spare key was, so he let himself in and crashed on the couch. However, when we agreed, we didn't know that we would have the girls to deal with. Aiden insisted we bring them here, since they're both three sheets to the wind and in no shape to care for themselves or each other. I agreed, but now that we're here, it hits me, *Is she going to sleep with him?*

I get my answer once Allison finishes her water; Aiden helps her out of her chair and starts guiding her down the hall to his room.

What the fuck! I assist Hailey to my room and step out into the hall while she changes. She insisted on keeping clothes here just for this occasion when she moved on campus. There was no point in arguing with her. I figured she'd need them at some point. Aiden steps out into the hall at the same time. I scowl at him.

"What's up, man?" Aiden asks, confused.

"Are you sleeping in the bed with her?" I growl at him.

Aiden laughs out loud. "Dude, she's like my sister, I've told you this."

I just stare at him. Deep down I know I'm being irrational, but the thought of her in another man's bed pisses me the fuck off, even if it is her 'brother'. "Maybe we should let the girls take my room and you and I can bunk together. I'll take the floor." I want Allison in my bed, even if it is Hailey she shares it with. I don't want her curled up with Aiden, but I don't want to think about that particular issue right now.

"No, man, it's cool. Ash and I have shared a bed before, just like you and Hales. She's changing now, and then we're just going to hit the sack."

Before I can reply, I hear Allison. "Ace, I'm done."

With that, Aiden walks back into his room and shuts the door. I stand here for several minutes before Hales steps out into the hall. "What are you doing?"

"Nothing." I stomp back into my room and slam the door.

Hailey joins me a few minutes later and climbs into bed. "Liam, are you okay?" she whispers.

I roll over and ignore her.

"Liam." She places her hand on my arm.

She's sitting up in bed when I look over my shoulder. I sigh and roll over. "What is it, Hales? I'm tired."

She studies me. "What happened to get you so pissed off all of a sudden?"

I stare at her, debating on what I should say. Should I tell her I'm mad as hell Allison is sleeping in Aiden's bed? Do I tell her Allison is all I can think about since meeting her yesterday? Do I tell her I feel like my world is spiraling out of control? No, I can't tell her any of those things. I'm not so sure she'd believe me anyway. Hell, I'm having a hard time wrapping my head around it. *I'm losing my fucking mind!*

"I'm fine, Hales, go to sleep."

"Liam, come on, I'm your sister. I know you better than that."

"Hailey," I warn her.

"I'm not ten anymore, Liam. You don't intimidate me. What the hell happened between the kitchen and now?" she continues to question me.

"Drop it, Hales, I mean it."

"No. Tell me what's up with you. We were all having a great time, and now all of a sudden you're Mr. Pissed-Off, and I want to know why," she insists.

"Fine, you want to know what's wrong. Allison, that's what's wrong, okay? Now. Go. To. Sleep."

Hailey looks confused. "Allison? Why, what did she do to you? She's the nicest person I know."

"Fuck," I grumble. "She won't get out of my head," I admit as I pull my pillow over my head.

There's complete silence following my outburst, and I think that maybe I'm lucky and Hailey has decided to leave well enough alone and has fallen asleep. I pull the pillow from my face and look over at her. She is staring at me. "You like her, don't you?"

"No...yes...Fuck, Hales, I don't know, okay?"

Hailey's grin spreads across her face. "Hot damn, I knew when you finally fell, it would be hard. I never dreamed I would have a front row seat in the action."

"What the hell are you talking about?"

"You, dumbass. You refuse to get serious about anyone. All that matters to you is football. You hook-up. You get a reputation as a player and you keep at it, like it's no big thing as long as you get yours and have football." Hailey nudges my shoulder. "Until now, that is," she adds, still grinning like the cat that ate the fucking canary.

She isn't done. "Not only do I get to witness this wondrous revelation take place, but since it just so happens to be with my roommate, I'll get an up close and personal view of my big brother, the player, falling for a girl."

"What? That's crazy. I'm not falling for her. I'm just extremely attracted to her, that's all. It's been a while since I've hooked up. I just need to remedy that and all will be back to normal. So, don't go spouting off crazy shit like that. You don't know what you're talking about."

"Whatever you say, big brother, whatever you say." Hailey smiles as she rolls over and falls asleep.

I lie here, for what seems like hours, staring at the shadows on the ceiling. My mind keeps drifting back to Allison and her gorgeous dark brown hair, and those big, beautiful, emerald green eyes. I also think about her being wrapped up in Aiden's arms and feel resentment sweep over me. It's almost four in the morning the last time I look at the clock before falling asleep.

A few hours later, my internal clock wakes me up. I'm used to getting up early to either run or hit the gym. I slip out of bed, careful not to wake Hailey. I'll let her sleep a little longer, but we have to be at our parents' house for lunch at one.

I walk down the hall to the bathroom to relieve myself, before heading to the kitchen to make a pot of coffee. I glance over at the couch and discover Blitzen has already left. As I walk into the kitchen, I have to blink to make sure my eyes aren't deceiving me. Allison is standing at the sink, looking out the window. She's wearing nothing but Aiden's football jersey. My feet are glued to the floor. My heart is pounding. Allison is the most beautiful girl I've ever seen. She must hear my racing heart because she turns around and offers me a shy smile.

"Sorry, I hope I didn't wake you up. I couldn't sleep. Aiden's a bed hog." She smiles and holds up her cell phone. "I took the opportunity to call and check on Gran."

And just like that my lust turns to annoyance. This beautiful, wonderful girl was sleeping in my best friend's bed, wearing his jersey. He says she's like family, but let's face it, they aren't related. What if he tried to touch her, and she's just blowing it off to protect him? *Aiden would never do that, would he?*

"Did he hurt you?" I ask her, concern lacing my voice.

Allison's mouth drops open in shock. "What? No, of course not. Aiden would never hurt me. He just likes to hog the bed, that's all."

I walk over to the sink and lean up against the counter facing her. Damn, this girl has a hold on me. I reach out and tuck a few loose strands of hair behind her ear. "It kills me to think of someone hurting you," I whisper to her. *What the fuck am I doing?* I questioned the morals of my best friend. I know Aiden would never lay a hand on a woman. My mind is all over the damn place. I need to get my shit together.

"H...He didn't hurt me, Liam. He wouldn't ever hurt me." She looks into my eyes, and I'm lost in her again. "Why would you think that?"

"I just—I feel like I need to protect you." I cup her cheek with the palm of my hand. "Do you feel this, Allison? This pull I'm feeling?" I ask her softly. "Please, tell me that I'm not alone in this—this overwhelming need to be close to you," I beg her.

Allison leans her face against my hand. "I don't really know what this feeling is, Liam. I-," she stops as if to collect her thoughts.

"Talk to me," I plead.

"I'm not as experienced as you. I've never been in a relationship, never been on a date." She laughs softly. "Unless you count Aiden at his family functions. I don't know what this is." She brings her hand up to cover mine against her cheek. "I know I can't be just a hookup. I know, even though I don't have the experience, I want more than physical. You can't give me that." She closes her eyes. It almost seems like it pains her to say that to me.

"Allison," I breathe and rest my forehead against hers, "you deserve love and commitment, and nothing less." I swallow the lump in my throat.

"I want that. I want to love someone with all that I am. It would be nice to have those feelings returned," she whispers to me. "I feel it too, Liam. I just don't know how to explain it, or what to do with it. I can't settle for meaningless."

"I know, baby, and I don't want you to." I kiss her forehead and back away. I immediately feel the loss. This girl is wreaking havoc on my senses and my emotions. No sooner than I pull away, Aiden walks into the kitchen. He walks straight to Allison and kisses her cheek.

"Morning, Ash," he mumbles as he makes himself a cup of coffee. "Mac, you headed out for a run?" he asks me.

"Yeah, I'll see you guys later." I gulp down the rest of my coffee, burning my tongue, and head out the door. I'm turned on beyond belief. I'm pissed off he gets to be close to her, and I'm pissed off because I can't have her for myself. I don't have time for a relationship, and she deserves nothing less.

CHAPTER NINE

Allison

"DID I JUST INTERRUPT SOMETHING?" Aiden asks me after Liam leaves for his run.

"No," I say, shaking my head. "Why would you ask that?"

"It just seemed, I don't know, tense in here."

"Liam and I were just chatting. He'd only been up a few minutes, actually, before you came out." I take a sip of my coffee. "I called Gran, she seems to be doing okay. I wanted to go home and see her today, but she says some ladies from church already planned to stop by and keep her company, so I guess I'll just stick around the dorm and hang out." I'm trying to change the subject. I'm not sure how I feel about what just happened with Liam. Something passed between us. I do feel this magnetic pull toward him, but I also meant what I said; I want it all, not just sex.

"Ash, I'm sure that Gran is fine. I'll call Mom and have her go over later and check on her, which I'm sure she already planned on doing anyway."

I nod and continue to drink my coffee.

"Listen, about Liam. He's my best friend, aside from you. He isn't the relationship type. I know he'd never hurt you intentionally, but be careful, okay?"

"I know he's not the king of commitment, but there's something about him." I shake my head to clear my thoughts. "It's like we're drawn to each other. I can't explain it."

Aiden walks over to where I'm standing and places his now empty cup in the sink. "I can see the sparks coming off the two of you. Just be careful, I would hate to see get you hurt."

"I will, and thank you for looking out for me," I say as I lean up to kiss him on the cheek. "Now, I'm going to go wake Hailey so we can head back to the dorms."

After several attempts and the promise of caffeine and bagels, Hailey finally gets out of bed, and we make our way back to our dorm. We're both still worn out from the alcohol and not sleeping in our own beds the night before. My mind keeps wandering back to my conversation with Liam. I was honest when I told him I feel it too. What exactly 'it' is, I'm not sure. I was also honest when I said I want it all or at least the intent for more. I need to learn how to control myself around him. How to not get lost in those blue eyes of his. *Ugh!*

"Earth to Allison." Hailey's sitting on her bed, watching me.

"Sorry, I spaced out. What's up?"

"I asked you if you wanted to come to my parents' for lunch. I know you were going to go home and see Gran, but since your plans changed, I want you to meet my parents," Hailey chirps as she bounces on her bed.

"I don't know, I hate to intrude."

Hailey waves her hand at me. "Not gonna happen. My parents are awesome, and they would love to meet my new roomie."

"Well, okay, if you're sure."

"Absolutely. We need to leave here around noon," Hailey advises me.

"Crap, that's twenty minutes. I need to get a move on." I grab some shorts, a tank, a matching set of my new undies and head to the shower. I rush through the shower and dress quickly. I use the blow dryer on my hair for a few minutes, then decide to let my natural wave air dry the rest of the way. I slap on some mascara and lip gloss, and I'm good to go. I walk out of our bathroom and Hailey whistles.

"Wow, you look amazing," she gushes.

"These shorts aren't as short as last night's, but they're close. Are you sure this is okay? I don't look sleazy, do I?"

"Hell no, you look hot." She grins.

I grab a pair of flip-flops from my closet just as there's a knock on the door. Hailey looks at me in question, and I shrug my shoulders. She hops off her bed to go open the door, while I go back into the bathroom to grab the watch I'd left on the sink. When I step out, my eyes immediately meet his. Liam. We continue to stare at one another, like we're the only two people in existence.

"Hey, Liam stopped to offer me a ride. He and Aiden are going to my parents' as well." Hailey smirks.

"Oh—um, well, I guess I'm ready." I grab my phone and wristlet off of my desk and meet them at the door. Hailey's out the door in a flash, yelling something about fighting Aiden for shotgun.

Liam smiles down at me. "Hey, you look beautiful today."

I offer him a shy smile. I can feel my face blush. "Thank you."

Liam bends down to whisper in my ear, "Now even more so. That blush on your face makes you even sexier."

I turn my head, trying to avoid him seeing my face. I can feel the burn; I probably look like a damn tomato. Liam places his hand on the small of my back and leads me out. "I'm sorry. I didn't mean to embarrass you. I just want you to know how I see you."

I simply nod my head and continue to walk to his SUV. I can feel the heat from his hand, not to mention, the after effects of his sexy voice when he whispered in my ear. I'm lucky I was able to nod. When Hailey asked me to join her at her parents', I never thought about Liam being there, let alone him driving us. I need to get my hormones in check. When we reach his Pathfinder, Hailey is in the back seat and Aiden is in the front passenger seat; obviously she lost the shotgun battle. Liam opens the door for me and waits until I'm buckled in to close the door and take his spot behind the wheel.

Aiden turns to greet me. "Hey, Ash, how are you feeling?"

"I'm good to go, so next time out I'm getting the full experience." I smile at him. Aiden just shakes his head and turns back around. I glance up to catch Liam looking at me in the rearview mirror. His gaze is intense. I turn my head to look out the window. I can't look into those blue eyes a minute longer and not combust. My hormones are on overload, and I need to cool down, clear my head.

Hailey and Aiden begin talking about the new Three Days Grace song playing on the radio and I'm about to comment that "Chalk Outline" is becoming one of my favorites when I feel my phone vibrate. I look down to see a message from Hailey. I look over at her and she smiles. I swipe the screen to unlock my phone and open her message.

HAILEY: Holy shit! My panties are wet just from being in the same damn car.

ME: What??

HAILEY: You know what I'm talking about.

ME: It's nothing just flirting.

HAILEY: I know my bro he's into you. He is NEVER like this.

.   .   .

ME: Come on we both know that's not true.

HAILEY: He opened your fucking door. Liam does NOT open doors!!!

I LOOK over at Hailey and roll my eyes. She immediately starts typing on her phone.

HAILEY: Wanna bet?

I SHAKE MY HEAD NO.

Hailey leans over and whispers in my ear, "It's going to be so much fun watching you both fall. Loser treats the winner to a day at the spa." She falls back against the seat giggling. *Is it too late to request a new roommate?*

This gets both Aiden and Liam's attention. Aiden turns around. "What are you two up to back there?"

"Oh, nothing. Allison and I are just making a little wager, that's all."

"Really? What kind of wager are we talking?" Liam asks as he meets my gaze in his rearview mirror. I feel my face instantly heat.

Aiden chuckles. "From the blush on Ash's face, I can only assume it involves the male species or sex. Maybe both."

"Aiden!" I shout as I reach up and smack him on the arm.

Aiden and Hailey are both roaring with laughter while Liam stares at the road in front of him. I can see his jaw twitch in the mirror. *Great, now he's pissed off at me.*

The rest of the drive is uneventful. I pretty much keep quiet, as does Liam. Aiden and Hailey continue their conversations about music and school. Liam and I answer questions, but both of us stay pretty quiet the remainder of the trip.

When we arrive, both of their parents are waiting for us on the porch. Liam, Aiden, and Hailey are all quick to get out of the car. I reach for my handle as the door flies open. Liam's standing there, holding his hand out to me, offering me assistance. I take his hand as he helps me down. I smile up at him. "Thank you."

Liam simply nods his head. Before I know what is happening, Hailey grabs me by the arm and starts pulling me to the porch. "Mom, Dad, this is my roommate, Allison. Allison, this is my mom and dad, Lisa and Rodney MacCoy."

I'm expecting a hand shake, but Hailey's mom pulls me into a hug. "It's so nice to meet you. Welcome, and, please, call me Mom or Lisa," she says as she releases me.

Their dad is just as friendly, he also gives me a quick hug. "Dad will work just fine for me as well." He smiles at me.

"It's nice to meet both of you. Thank you for having me."

"You're welcome here anytime. Now, I hope you all are hungry. I made homemade lasagna, salad, and garlic bread. For dessert I made dirt cake," Lisa tells us.

"Did I hear dirt cake?" Aiden asks as he walks up on the porch. He goes straight for Mrs. MacCoy and hugs her. "You spoil me, woman."

Mrs. MacCoy just laughs as she hugs Liam. "I just like to keep my family fed, and if it happens to be their favorite foods, so be it," she says, smiling at the four of us.

Liam and Aiden shake hands and man hug with Mr. MacCoy as Hailey shuffles us into the house. Their home reminds me a lot of the Emersons'. Family pictures line the walls, throws thrown over the back of the couch. It feels lived in, happy. It's been years since Gran's house felt happy. The living room now houses Gran's hospital bed, as it's too hard for her to get up the stairs to any of the bedrooms. The kitchen counters are lined with bottle after bottle of her prescription medications. I feel an ache in my chest thinking about Gran. I just spoke to her this morning, and she says she's doing fine, but I know her health is failing, and I feel like the worst granddaughter in the world being off at school while she's home alone.

"Earth to Allison," Hailey says as she waves her hands back and forth in front of my face.

"Oh, sorry," I say as she pulls me out of my thoughts. "I was just thinking about Gran. I feel bad not being with her each day," I explain.

Aiden walks over to me and pulls me into a hug. "I talked to Mom before we left, and she said Gran is fine and she'll check on her again later today. Gran wants you to enjoy life, Ash. Please, try not to worry." He kisses me on the forehead, and I hug him tighter.

CHAPTER TEN

Liam

I HAVE to get out of here. To see Aiden kiss her good morning, even though it's just a peck on the cheek, irritates me. My annoyance is back full force. It's bad enough I have to see her wearing his jersey, but to see him touch her, it's killing me. She feels it too, she told me that much, but she wants more. I've never done more. I've never had a girlfriend, I never wanted one. I have football. The draft is coming up in less than a year. My dream, since I was old enough to hold a football, has been to play in the NFL. I can't lose focus on that now. However, my mind and my heart, yes, my heart, did not get the fucking memo. I've never had a girl hold my interest for longer than a few hours, how could I possibly give Allison more?

When I get back to the apartment, after my run, the girls are gone. I feel both relief and sadness. Thinking about how long it'll be before I see her again, I get an idea in my head. I'll surprise Hailey and pick her up for lunch at our parents'. Hopefully, Allison will be in their dorm room when I get there. It'll be a quick glimpse, but at this point I'll take what I can get. Checking the time, I rush through my shower, then I meet Aiden in the living room. "Hey, man, ready to go?"

He nods as he gets off the couch. "Little earlier than we usually leave?" He raises his eyebrows, questioning me.

I shrug my shoulders. "Yeah, I need to stop and pick up Hales, no sense in both of us driving there when we're only minutes away from each other." I try to sound as nonchalant as possible. Inside I'm screaming for him to hurry the fuck up. I need to see Allison.

He just stares at me. "Come on, man, what's really going on?" he questions me.

"Nothing, it just makes more sense for me to pick her up, that's all," I reply as I continue tying my shoes.

"Did you know that Allison is coming today?"

I whip my head around to look at him. "She is?" I feel my heart rate pick up at just the thought of being able to be in the same car with her for any length of time. "Are you sure?"

He nods. "I'm positive." Letting out a deep sigh he continues, "Please, tell me you aren't going after her."

I hesitate before answering, "She wants more."

"She deserves more."

"You think I don't fucking know that? Don't you think I would give her the world if I could?" I sneer at him.

Aiden stares at me as if he is trying to decipher what I just said. "She's really gotten to you, hasn't she?"

"Yes...no...hell, I don't even know anymore." I place my elbows on my knees and lean over with my hands covering my face. "What I do know is since I met her I can't stop thinking about her. When I'm near her, I feel this intense attraction that I've never felt. I want to protect her. Hell, this morning I wanted to rip your fucking head off for kissing her on the cheek."

"I really want to see where this goes, man. I need to work out these feelings." I stand up and pace the floor. "I know she's like a sister to you, and you've told me multiple times there's nothing going on, but speak now, man, if there's more. I plan on seeing where this attraction goes. And before you go ape shit, if you want her, I'll back off, but that's the only damn thing that will keep me from trying to work out these feelings I have for her." The words are out of my mouth before I know what I'm saying. I realize I mean every word. Aiden's words flash through my mind *"She deserves better, she deserves respect and love."*

"Liam, you and Allison both mean a lot to me. Do.Not.Hurt.Her. I'll support you as long as you agree she's *not* a fuck buddy. She's special and needs to be treated that way. Think about Hailey and how you would feel about her being treated like a quick fuck."

I nod my head, understanding what he's telling me. Allison really is like a sister to him, and he wants to protect her. Problem is so do I, and I'm not sure just how to deal with all of these emotions running rampant through me. Can I deal with giving her more? Can I deal with the close relationship they share? If I'm going to give her more, she's going to be mine.

Aiden senses I'm hanging by a thread and changes the subject as we make our way out to my Pathfinder. "So, what's on the menu for today?"

I laugh. "Not sure, but you know Mom. Whatever it is, there'll be an abundance of it and it'll be delicious." I hand him my phone. "Text Hales and let her know we're coming to get them." The plan was to surprise her and try to catch a glimpse of Allison. However, now that Allison is going, I need to make sure she doesn't leave before I get there.

Taking my phone, he nods and proceeds to text Hales and let her know we'll be taking them to Mom and Dad's.

Aiden stays in the car while I go up to get the girls. I knock on the door and Hales answers. "Hey, you guys ready?" Before she can answer, Allison comes walking out of the bathroom. She's wearing jean shorts and a tank top with flip-flops. I want her. She looks surprised to see me. Hailey must have seen the question in her eyes, so she starts explaining Aiden and I are also going to our parents' for lunch and we're all riding together.

Hailey's already out the door, talking about who is riding shotgun. I can only hope it'll be Allison. Although, I know, I'm not that lucky. Allison walks over to me, and, without even thinking, I lean down to tell her how beautiful she looks. I pull back as I catch her scent. Not able to control myself, I place my hand on the small of her back and lead her out to my SUV. I open the door for her and wait until she's settled in before closing it.

I'm not lucky enough to have Allison beside me in the front seat, but she's sitting directly behind me, and I keep glancing at her in my rearview mirror. She has her hair hanging loose over her shoulders. Yep, she's beautiful. She doesn't need makeup, she just needs to be Allison. I grip the steering wheel tighter and focus on the road. She wants more, I've never done more. Can I focus on her and football, not to mention, school? If there's ever a reason to try, it would be for Allison, she's intoxicating. This is the same question that has been running through my mind all day. I told Aiden I was going to see where this goes, and I want that. I also don't want to hurt her. My head is a jumbled mess.

The conversation is flowing; I listen, trying to remain focused on the road and not on Allison. All of a sudden, I hear Hailey giggling like a school girl, which pulls me out of my thoughts. Aiden asks them what they are up to. Hailey says that she and Allison have a bet going. I'm intrigued.

Allison and Hailey are laughing and talking about some type of wager, and I'm fine until Aiden mentions it involving the male species, someone other than me. Then I'm instantly pissed off. I need to get a grip, but I can't seem to control it when it comes to her.

Allison leans forward and punches Aiden in the arm at his teasing. I clench my jaw tight and turn my focus back to the road. It pisses me off beyond comprehension to hear the words male and sex mentioned with Allison. Just the thought of her with anyone else has me seeing red. The thought of someone else kissing those sweet lips, running their hands through her beautiful locks, touching her soft skin...*Fuck.*

We pull into my parents' drive, and I hop out of the SUV. I open Allison's door and offer my hand to help her out. She grabs my hand, and, in that instance, I feel all the anger I'm feeling fade. As soon as she steps out, Hales is dragging her by the hand up the steps to meet our parents. Thoughts of her being here with me as mine flash through my mind. I should be the one introducing my girl to my parents, not my sister. *My girl? What the fuck is she doing to me?*

I watch as my parents embrace Allison and welcome her to our home. She smiles her heart stopping smile, and I can tell they love her already. Aiden was right, she's easy to love. Not that I'm in love with her, but she's easy to like I guess that's a better way of putting it. Hailey leads us all inside as Aiden talks to my mother about his love for her cooking and desserts.

As we gather around the table, Allison gets a faraway look in her eyes. Before I know what's happening, Aiden walks over to her, whispers in her ear, and pulls her close as he kisses the top of her head. *Why the fuck does he keep touching her?* I slam the salad bowl down on the table, which causes me to be on the receiving end of questioning looks from both of my parents.

Aiden returns to his seat. "This looks great, Mrs. Mac, thanks again for having us."

"You know you're always welcome," Mom tells him.

"So, can you believe Allison and Aiden grew up living next door to each other? Small world, huh?" Hailey says as she fills her plate with lasagna.

"Really, are you two dating?" This question coming from my mother. I happen to be taking a drink when she asks this and begin to cough, her question not sitting well with me. No matter how many times Aiden tells me they're just friends, like siblings, he still touches her intimately. I hate every second of it. I want to be the one to wrap my arms around her.

Aiden laughs. "No, Allison and I are best friends." He looks at me. "She's like my little sister."

My mom looks at Allison. "So, you're Ash?" she questions. Aiden has pretty much been a permanent fixture at my house whenever I'm here. He has talked a lot about Allison or 'Ash', as he calls her.

"Yes, we call each other by our initials. It's something we started when we were really young. I moved in with my gran when I was ten. I lost my parents in a car crash. I was scared and lonely." She looks at Aiden and smiles. "Ace here made sure I knew my way around school and we bonded. We've been best friends ever since." Allison discretely wipes a tear that's starting to escape. It takes everything in me not to wrap her in my arms. The thought that she's sad or hurt rips my heart out.

"I'm so sorry about your parents, dear," my mom tells Allison. "I didn't mean to pry."

"No, it's fine. It was a long time ago," Allison replies. "May I use your restroom?" she asks softly.

Hailey speaks up, "Of course, it's the last door down the hall on your right."

Allison leaves the table, and I release the breath I'm holding.

"You alright, son?" my dad asks.

I nod, not wanting to get into the fact that Allison has me tied in knots. That the thought of her in pain is making my arms ache to hold her.

After a few minutes Hailey says, "I'm going to go check on her."

"No." I stand from the table. "Let me do it." I quickly excuse myself and head down the hall. I know that I, as well as Allison, are going to be the topic of conversation, but I can't bring myself to care. I want to be there for her.

I stop in front of the bathroom door and lean my forehead against it. I can hear her soft cries. I knock softly. "Allison, it's Liam. Can you let me in, sweetheart?"

"Just give me a minute, I'll be fine," she chokes out.

"Please," I whisper.

I hear her shuffling toward the door and then hear the handle turn. When she pulls the door open, her face is blotchy and her eyes are red and swollen. Without even thinking, I step inside and shut the door. I pull her close to me and wrap her in my arms. I kiss the top of her head, and as I do, she begins to cry harder. I'm not sure how long we stay like this, but while I'm holding her I lose a piece of myself to Allison Shay Hagan.

She pulls away from me slowly. "Sorry about your shirt," she whispers.

I pull her chin up with my thumb and forefinger, so she's looking me in the eye. "Are you okay? Do you want to talk about it?"

She shakes her head. "I feel like such a baby. It was years ago, I should be able to talk about it."

"Is there something in particular that upset you?" I ask softly as I hug her back to my chest and slowly rub my hand up and down her back.

"Not really, it's just..." she sniffles.

"What, baby, what happened?"

"It's just family dinners. I miss those, for the last eight years it's just been Gran and me."

I can't get words to pass through the lump in my throat. My only reply is to pull her tighter. As I do, she in turn wraps her arms tight around my waist. After getting my emotions under control, I pull away from her and cup her face in my hands. I wipe her tears away with my thumbs. "You are amazing, you have so many people who love you, Aiden, his parents, Hailey. My parents adore you." I swallow back my emotions. "You have me," I whisper, never tearing my eyes from hers.

"Liam," she murmurs.

Her plea sends me over the edge, and I slowly bring her face to mine as I lean down. I stare at her lips and then back to her eyes, letting her know my intent. I need to kiss her more than I need my next breath. I wait, as my intentions set in, I can see when under-standing flashes across her face, she licks her lips. I lean a little closer, closing the space between us. Hesitating, giving her the opportunity to stop me.

She doesn't.

When my lips touch hers, I feel the tremor in my hands, which are gently holding her close to me. She must have felt it too because she places her hands over mine as I continue to caress her cheeks while I kiss her. She opens her mouth, and I slip my tongue inside. The taste of her on my tongue causes me to release a deep moan, and as I do Allison slows the kiss and rests her forehead against my chest.

"Liam."

"Mmm." Again I'm at a loss for words. I have kissed my share of girls and not once did any of those kisses elicit this kind of reaction from me. I've never in my life felt this kind of connection with any other human being.

"What are we doing?"

I kiss her forehead before I pull back to look her in the eye. "I was kissing the most amazing girl I've ever met." I need her to know she's different from anyone else I've ever been with.

She blushes. "I want more, Liam. Not that I expect a proposal next week, but you've already made it clear you won't make a commitment, so what are we doing?"

I shake my head and pull her back to my chest. "I don't know, baby. All that I can tell you is that kiss was incomparable to anything I've ever felt. You wreck me, you know that?" I ask, searching her face for understanding.

"Well, since that was officially my first kiss, I don't have anything to compare it to, but this feeling," she grabs my hand and lays it over her heart, "this connection that makes my heart race is uncharted waters for me. I wish I could hold onto it and never let go," she sighs, "but I need all of you, Liam. I don't want to share you, and I can't just be a fling. My heart can't take it." She brushes her hand across my cheek. "If you ever decide you can give me all of you, you know where to find me." She lifts up on her tiptoes and gives me one last chaste kiss on the lips. "Thank you for listening...and for the kiss," she says as she turns and walks out of the room.

I stand here, trying to regain control of my emotions while her words race through my mind.

CHAPTER ELEVEN

Allison

WHEN I HEAR the knock on the door and then Liam's voice, I cry harder. I'm so embarrassed I didn't control my emotions in front of everyone. My parents have been gone for a long time. I should be able to tell people about them without turning into a blubbering idiot. I'm missing Gran, and to see Liam and Hailey so carefree with their parents, even Aiden, I lost it. I just need a minute to get myself under control. When I hear Liam's whispered, "Please," I find myself opening the door. As soon as he sees me, he steps into the room, shuts the door, and wraps me in his strong arms. I feel safe and content, that feeling isn't one I have much experience with. I always feel like I'm waiting for the other shoe to drop.

Liam holds me tight as I attempt to explain my breakdown. After a few minutes, he tells me I'm amazing and I have Aiden and his parents, as well as Hailey and their parents. After a short pause, he also tells me I have him. That simple statement sends heat surging throughout my body. What I wouldn't give to have this man be mine.

To always know he'd be there to wrap me in his arms and cherish me, just like he's doing at this exact moment, as if I'm the most important person in his life.

"Liam," is all I'm able to get out, my mind is reeling. I want him to want me. I want to be enough for him. I want all of him. There's no way I'll settle for less.

The connection we have is unexplainable. I look into his eyes and the want I see there mirrors my own. He leans in closer, and I know he's going to kiss me. I want him to kiss me, just this once. I'll take his kiss as a token of what I can never have. Liam is a no commitment, sexy football god. I'm one of many women who swoons over him daily. As he leans in closer, I can feel his breath against my face. He hesitates, and I know he's expecting me to stop him, but I don't, I want this. I want my first kiss to be Liam, a reminder of this over-whelming chemistry flowing between us. I lick my lips and within seconds his lips touch mine. Liam has my face cupped gently in his hands. I feel him start to tremble. I place my hands over his as he deepens the kiss. I open my mouth, inviting him in, and he takes full advantage. Once his tongue slips in I hear him growl deep in his throat, and I know I need to stop this. I want him, and he is unattain-able in my eyes, and we have to stop.

"Liam," I breathe. "What are we doing?"

Liam kisses my forehead as he proceeds to tell me he's *'kissing the most amazing girl he has ever met'*. I melt and right then I lose a piece of my heart to him. I know he can never be mine, but he has a part of me, which is crazy because we just met; all I know is he just does. I'm glad I'm still in his arms, or I would be a puddle of lust on the bath-room floor.

I can feel his chest rising and falling. I can feel the steady beat of his heart. I look up into his eyes, getting lost in a sea of deep blue emotions. He proceeds to tell me our kiss is basically the best kiss of his existence. My resolve is beginning to crumble. I'm so tempted to throw caution to the wind and have a fling with Liam. Instead, I put on my big girl panties and do the responsible thing. I tell him if he ever decides he can give me all of him, he knows where to find me. I give him one final quick kiss on the lips and leave him there in the bathroom.

I walk back into the kitchen and take my seat next to Hailey. She looks at me in question and I shrug my shoulders. She smiles at me, like she just discovered the cure for cancer. I pick up my fork and continue to eat. It's Aiden who breaks the tension.

"Ash, you have got to taste Mrs. Mac's dirt cake," he says as he shovels in a humongous bite.

Mrs. Mac smiles at me. "Would you like a bowl?"

"Yes, please, dinner was great." I stand up to carry my now empty plate to the kitchen.

Liam appears at my side. "I got it," as he grabs my plate and walks to the kitchen. Mr. Mac stands to follow him.

The remainder of the day is uneventful. We all sit down to play a game of Back Alley Thirteen, Liam, Aiden, and Mr. Mac play their guitars and we all sing. We laugh and joke until it's time to leave. Aiden and Hailey keep giving me questioning looks. I smile at them to let them know I'm good. Liam continues to dote on me, grabbing me drinks, holding my chair for me, and such. All of my senses are on high alert. When we leave, he holds the door for me again and helps me into the back seat of his Pathfinder. The drive back is quiet, since we're all full and worn out. When we arrive at the dorm, Liam hops out and opens my door for me. I smile and say, "Thank you". I give Aiden a hug, then link arms with Hailey as we head to our room.

We're barely through the doors of the building before Hailey pounces on me for information.

"What the fuck was that?" she says with a huge smile on her face.

I look at her as if she is crazy. "What was what?" I can tell she isn't buying my poor attempt to evade her questions.

"Don't play dumb with me, Allison Hagan. What is that chemistry between you and my brother? Holy shit, sparks were flying all damn day."

"You're crazy, there were no sparks. Liam was just being...nice, that's all," I say, my voice cracking. *Yeah, that was real convincing.*

"I call bullshit. What you're forgetting is he's my brother, and I know him all too well. Never in my life have I seen him be attentive to any girl, unless he was trying to hook up. He ran from the table to chase after you and see if you were okay. Then he was in the bathroom with you for a while." She smirks.

I throw myself down on my bed and cover my head with my pillow. I contemplate how much I should tell her. Liam is her brother after all, but she's my roommate, and I need someone to talk to about all of this. Aiden would never understand. I take a deep breath, remove the pillow, and say, "We kissed," and quickly cover my face back up.

"I knew it!"

Before I know what's happening, Hailey's on my bed, pulling the pillow away. "You kissed him?" she questions.

Unable to speak and feeling the heat engulf my cheeks, I nod my head yes and look up at the ceiling.

"This is awesome. Wouldn't it be great if you guys ended up getting married? We would be sisters for real."

"Seriously, you're not mad, or think this is weird?"

"Well, when things start to heat up with you two spare me the graphic details, but no, I'm cool with it. Liam is a great guy, he just has his priorities all out of whack. I would love to see him get serious and what better person than my new roomie-BFF?"

"I'm sorry to disappoint, but it doesn't mean anything. Liam has made it clear he would never consider a relationship, and I don't want to waste my time on a fling, so it's never gonna happen with us."

Hailey laughs. "Oh, it's so gonna happen, just like I told you earlier. I'm going to enjoy watching this play out. The show so far has been AH-MAZING," she sings as she hops back to her bed.

THE FIRST WEEK of classes goes smoothly. Hailey and I'd already mapped out where we needed to go, so we could ensure we'd be on time. That's yet another thing she and I have in common, neither one of us like to be late. Thursday night we're hanging out in our room trying to figure out how to celebrate our first week. Neither one of us has classes on Friday, so we'll have a three-day weekend for this semester. *Hell yeah.* I haven't seen Liam at all this week. Of course, I've gone out of my way to avoid him and Aiden. I gave Aiden the excuse I was busy with diving into my classes. He bought it, thankfully.

My cell phone starts singing LMFAO "Sexy and I Know It." Aiden's ringtone. He programmed it himself. He's quite proud of his selection and often calls when we're together just to remind me.

"Hey, Ace," I chirp.

"Hey, you. What are you and Hales up to tonight?" he asks.

"Well, we were actually just discussing that. How about you?" I want to say how about you and Liam, but I don't want to be obvious. It's been a week since I've seen him.

"Nothing really. Liam and I are just sitting around, thinking about going out for pizza, and wanted to see if you and Hales wanted to come with?"

I pull the phone away from my ear. "Hey, Hales, Aiden said he and Liam are going out for pizza and they want to know if we want to come with."

"Yes. How much time do we have?" she responds as she jumps off her bed and starts rummaging through her closet.

I laugh at her antics. "Yeah, we're in. Where do you want to meet?" I listen to Aiden tell me he and Liam will pick us up in twenty minutes. I quickly say goodbye, so I can get ready.

"They'll be here in twenty minutes to pick us up," I tell Hailey as I laugh at her throwing clothes around our room.

"Get your ass in gear, missy. We only have twenty minutes, make that nineteen. What are you going to wear?"

I shrug my shoulders. I'm a what-you-see-is-what-you-get kind of girl. I want Liam to want me, but I want him to want the real me. I refuse to pretend to be someone I'm not in order to earn his affections. "What's wrong with what I have on?" I question her.

Hailey rolls her eyes at me. "Nothing, I just think you should change it up a little is all. My brother is chomping at the bit for you, and we just want to give him the little push he needs."

"What do you mean he's chomping at the bit for me?" I question her, hands on my hips.

She sighs. "He's called and texted me more this week than he has in our entire lives. He wanted to make sure you were okay after Sunday."

"Wow. Okay, well, I guess that's a good thing. I told him I wanted more, Hales. Do you think he'll ever be able to give me that? Give anyone that?" I ask her, sadness in my voice.

Hailey nods her head yes. "I do, he's really into you. Liam's just working through his emotions right now. He's never wanted anyone like this before, or cared how they were doing. This is all new to him. Give him time to adjust to the thought of being in a relationship." She brings a pair of distressed capri jeans and a spaghetti strap tank over to me. "Put these on with some flip-flops. They'll show off your curves, but it's still really casual, so it won't look like you're trying too hard."

I don't respond, instead I make quick work of changing my clothes, then let Hailey touch up my makeup and hair, which I'd straightened today. We barely finish when we hear a knock at the door.

"Come in!" we both yell at the same time as we giggle.

CHAPTER TWELVE

Liam

I PESTER the shit out of Aiden until he finally breaks down and calls Allison and invites her and Hailey out for pizza with us. Luckily, they agree, and soon Aiden and I are on our way up to their dorm room to pick them up. Aiden knocks on the door and a chorus of, "Come in," and a lot of giggling rings through the door.

Aiden turns the knob and walks in. I'm ready to lecture Hales on leaving her door unlocked, even though the dorm has security, but Aiden beats me to it. "Ash, what the fuck? Why in the hell was your door unlocked, and why did you just yell for us to come in without checking who it was first?" he asks her angrily, but you can also hear the concern in his voice.

Allison rolls those emerald eyes at him. "Chill out, Ace, don't go getting your feathers all ruffled. You said you would be here in twenty minutes, and it's been twenty-two, so I knew it was you. Besides, even if it wasn't you, I knew you and Liam were on your way."

"Allison," Aiden growls.

She walks up to him and gives him a hug. "Relax, Hales and I are fine, nothing is going to happen." She steps back and turns toward me.

"Hey, Liam," she says with a smile.

"Hey, you guys ready to go?" I ask her and Hailey, looking back and forth between the two of them. That's really my only option. If I stare at Allison any longer, I'm going to have huge issues in the land down under that I'll have to deal with. She's always gorgeous and tonight is no exception. She isn't dressed up, and, honestly, I think that's what makes her so fucking sexy. She's just Allison, beautiful sexy Allison—who wants more. I shake my head to clear my thoughts.

"Yep, we're good to go," Hailey says as she links her arm through mine. She leads us out of the dorm to Aiden's car.

Hailey looks behind us then leans into me. "She's really into you," she says with a smirk.

I raise an eyebrow in question.

"She is, she just doesn't want to be another notch. I think the two of you would be great together," she declares as she climbs into the front seat of Aiden's car.

Aiden and Allison reach the car and discover Hailey has claimed the shotgun position. Aiden shakes his head and laughs. He's used to her antics. I smile at Allison and shrug my shoulders as if to say, 'What do you do?'

She laughs and gets in the back seat. I follow suit and immediately I'm aware of how close we are to each other. Her hand rests on the seat mere inches from mine. I want to lace our fingers together. Fuck, if the guys could hear me now, I would so be handing over my man card. I can't understand why I'm so consumed by this girl. Well, that's not true. I can still feel her lips on mine, the taste of her on my tongue—fuck, I'm getting hard. I need to think of something else, or this is going to be a long ass night guaranteed to end in a cold shower.

We arrive at the pizza place and, luckily, it isn't packed yet. We make our way inside, and Hailey tells the hostess we prefer a booth.

She grabs Aiden's arm and drags him with her; he doesn't seem to mind. Hailey scoots into the booth and pulls Aiden down beside her, which leaves me to sit beside Allison. *God, I love my little sister.* I motion for Allison to slide in the booth, she does, and as she passes me, her hand brushes mine and I'm full-on hard in an instant. Just like that. A simple touch from this girl, and I have the ability to hammer nails with my cock. I slide in quickly, hoping to hide the evidence of what she does to me.

We all decide to share a pizza and bread sticks. Hailey decides we need a little get to know you session. She thinks it's a good idea for everyone to learn more about each other. She smiles sweetly at me. I know she's doing this to help me learn more about Allison. I've bugged the shit out of her this week. Conversation flows, and I actually learn a lot about Allison, and she about me, I'm sure. I learn her major is still undeclared and she struggled with going to college to begin with. Her favorite color is purple and her favorite flower is daisies. She loves all music from Nickelback to Taylor Swift. She enjoys scrapbooking, which she said is something she and her gran do together. The more I learn about her, the more I want her. I can't explain it, and at this point, I'm not sure I want to. She's real. She's not putting on a show, or trying to be something she's not to get my attention. She's just Allison.

Aiden and I go to the counter to pay. When we make it back to the booth, there are two punks in our seats. The punk beside Allison is leaning his shoulder into hers, obviously flirting with her. The other has his arm on the back of the booth behind Hales. I don't know the fuckers, but I recognize them from around campus. I'm channelling all of my inner calm, so I don't beat the shit out of these two. Aiden and I step up to the booth. Hailey's worried eyes meet mine. She knows I'm about to lose my shit.

"Hey, hun, are we all set?" Hailey asks Aiden. I'm not sure what she's playing at until Allison speaks up.

"Hey, babe, are you up for some ice cream?" she asks me with the sweetest smile on her face. I can see tension in her eyes. It's obvious these guys said or did something to make them uncomfortable.

The two douche bags actually look offended, like the girls were leading them on. They huff as they get up and make their way to the back of the restaurant. I clench my fists at my sides. I want to punch them, just once is all it would take with those two. I see Hailey grab Aiden's arm and lead him toward the door. He's having pretty much the same reaction as I am. I'm seething mad and turn to follow the two goons when I feel soft hands encircle my arm.

"Liam." That's all it takes. Her saying my name, like I'm all that matters in her world, and instantly my anger evaporates just as fast as it came on. Her soft voice and soft hands instantly calming me. I cup her face with my free hand and kiss her, just a chaste kiss, but it has to happen. I rest my forehead on hers. "Let's get that ice cream." I pull away and lead her out to the car.

We decide to go through the drive-thru at Dairy Queen for ice cream, and then drive to a nearby park to eat it. We all sit around the picnic tables laughing and talking. I'm having so much fun, I don't want to drop the girls back off at their dorm. Allison, however, is driving home to see her gran tomorrow, so she wants to get an early start. I'm bummed, but I understand. I know how important her gran is to her. We walk the girls to their dorm and remind them to lock the door. I don't get anymore kisses, but Aiden and I get hugs from both of them. At this point, I'll take what I can get. I'm starting to wonder if any amount of Allison Hagan will ever be enough.

When we get back to our apartment, I thank Aiden for getting the girls together with us and head to my room to shower. I'm lying on my bed staring at the ceiling, thinking about Allison, of course, when Aiden walks in. "Hey, man," I greet him.

"Hey, you turning in?" he asks me. Okay, something is up.

"Trying," I reply honestly. He knows this thing with Allison is tearing me up inside.

"Listen, man, I watched you tonight, you're different with her. Hell, all week you've been different, blowing girls off, not getting together with the guys. I can tell you're really into her, and, well, I just want you to know if you're serious, I'm good with it." He pauses to gauge my reaction. Of course, I'm speechless. "She really is just like my little sister. She's been through a lot, and I want to protect her," he shakes his head, "but the way you look at her, I've only ever seen that look one other time in my life."

"Really, and when was that?" I know how I look at her, like she's the most precious gift on the damn planet. I've tasted those lips and been subjected her hugs. No one compares to Allison.

Aiden waits for me to look at him. "My parents. You look at Allison the same way that my parents look at each other. Their love is deep and genuine, I see that when you look at her. Protect her and don't rush her, man. She deserves that and more."

I nod my head. "I would give her the world if I could." There's no need for me to elaborate. Aiden knows I'm struggling with my feelings for her. Even so, he just gave me his blessing. Now it's up to me to decide what I'm going to do with it. I told him I was pursuing her, yet I've hesitated. My mind is all over the place.

Aiden nods and turns, leaving me with my thoughts. I lie awake in bed for hours just thinking about life, football, and most of all, Allison. Can I fit a serious relationship in with all the other craziness of senior year, football, and the draft? Can I handle not having her in my life? I can feel the answer beating in my chest, but admitting it is a whole other feat. That's the question running through my mind as I drift off to sleep.

CHAPTER THIRTEEN

Allison

THE LAST TWO months have been a whirlwind. Hales and I have settled into a nice little routine with school and sharing space. We've spent a lot of time hanging out with Aiden and Liam, just as a group of friends. There've been no more kisses, but I do hug Liam hello and goodbye each time I see him, just like I do Aiden. It's hard to see him so much and not be with him. At least, I don't have to watch him date. Neither Aiden nor Liam have been on a date since the semester started, well, not as far as Hailey and I know of anyway. Hailey and I really haven't dated either. She went out on a date with that Todd guy when school first started, but they haven't gotten together since then due to their schedules. It could also be because Aiden and Liam always get to us first. I can't help but wonder if Aiden doesn't have a little crush on Hales, I know she has a crush him. I need to keep an eye on those two.

It's Friday night and Hales and I are staying in. Aiden and Liam are at an away game. Hailey and I never miss a home game, but the away games all depend on where they are. So tonight, we're having a girls' night. Just hanging out in our dorm, listening to music and consuming lots of junk food.

"So, Todd just texted me and wants to go out tomorrow night. I was thinking maybe you could come with me and double with his friend Jason?" Hailey asks me.

"I can't. I'm going home this weekend to spend some time with Gran."

"Please, Allie, you can leave early Sunday morning to go see Gran. Please, pretty please?"

"Fine," I say with a sigh. "What is this Jason guy like, anyway?" I ask her.

"He's hot, that's what he is." She laughs.

"Okay, so he's hot, does he go to Duke with Todd?"

"Yeah, he does." She pauses to collect her thoughts. "They both used to play football in high school. They played for our rival school. Liam really doesn't like either one of them. I don't really know why, he never said."

"Great," I groan. I don't want to piss Liam off. I want him to want me. Of course, I'm not going to admit that out loud. The last couple months we've flirted endlessly, and the four of us are now a package deal, but we're all just friends, siblings hanging out. There have been no more kisses.

"It'll be fun, trust me. Just four people hanging out, having a good time. I'll text Todd and let him know. I think we're going to go to The Warehouse, you cool with that?" she asks as her fingers fly across the screen of her phone.

"Um, do you know if Liam and Aiden will be there?" I question.

"Definitely not, or else I wouldn't go. I don't enjoy my brother when he's pissed off."

"Okay then, The Warehouse it is. I just hope Liam and Aiden don't show up. "

"I talked to Liam earlier; they're going to a party at Blitzen's. I'll text him, just to make sure."

CHAPTER FOURTEEN

Liam

This week has been crazy. This is my last year of college, football season is in full swing, and I haven't been able to stop thinking about Allison. I haven't so much as looked at another girl these past two months. The memory of her pressed tight against me and the taste of her lips on mine is on constant replay in my mind. This moment is a perfect example, I should be focusing on the mound of homework sitting in front of me, but I can't concentrate. All I see is Allison. My phone vibrates alerting me I have a new message.

Hailey: *Hey, big bro! How are your classes?*

Me: *Good, buried in a mound of homework. Yours?*

Hailey: *Good. Diff from high school.*

Me: *Yea. Also, a hell of a lot more fun.*

Hailey: *True. What are you guys up to this weekend?*

Me: *Blitzen is having a party. You?*

I am curious as to what she and Allison have planned for this weekend. However, I'm not sure that tidbit of knowledge is going to help my obsession. *What am I now, a fucking stalker?*

Hailey: *Not sure. Need to check with roomie.*

Me: You can come with us Saturday.

Why the fuck did I just do that? I need to stay away from Allison to get her out of my head. We've all been spending so much time together it's like my brain is set on the Allison show and it's a twenty-four hour, seven days a week marathon. I'm still struggling with this attraction I have for her. I thought maybe being around her would lessen the appeal, but it's had the opposite effect. I only want her more. I need to hook-up with someone. Yes, that would get me back on track. The only problem with that is, all I see is Allison. I haven't got laid since several weeks before I met her, not for the lack of available women. It seems everywhere I go there are beautiful women flirting with me or passing me their numbers, even when we are out with Hales and Allison. Hell, for all they know we're two couples, but that doesn't stop them. The only problem is I find myself comparing each and every damn one of them to Allison.

They don't measure up.

Hailey: Thanks, but I want to go dancing.

Me: You both be safe call if you need me. Don't go home with any losers.

Hailey: LOL! You guys too. Love you!

Me: Love you too.

Aiden walks in. "Hey, man, Blitzen just called and said the pipes burst in his apartment. The party tomorrow night is off. I told him he could crash here for a few days, you okay with that?"

"Damn, that sucks for him. Yeah, that's cool; the couch is his."

"So, any ideas for tomorrow night?" he asks me

"No, but I need to go out."

Aiden raises his eyebrow at me in question. "Any particular reason?" He plops down beside me on the couch.

I point to the stack of books on my lap and the coffee table. I don't need to tell him Allison is also embedded in my brain, and I need to focus on someone else to stop it. He knows how wound up she has me.

Aiden laughs. "No shit, I feel your pain." Choosing to ignore the fact we both know Allison is the real reason.

"Let's just go to The Warehouse," I suggest.

Aiden nods. "Old faithful. Sounds like a plan."

As soon as I walk into The Warehouse the next night, thoughts of that first night here with Allison and holding her close are front and center within my mind. I try to fight them off, but I'm losing the battle, slowly, painfully, as I relive every moment of that night. We push through the crowd to the bar and order a beer. Aiden spots Blitzen, so we head toward the two tables he and several of our teammates have pushed together. Aiden and I sit at the end of the table and easily slip into the conversation about Friday's practice. We're all chatting, drinking and having a good time when Mike, a defensive lineman, speaks up.

"Fuck, Mac, who is that hot ass chick with your sister?" he says as he tilts his head toward the dance floor.

I glance at Aiden as we both whip our heads around to see who he is looking at, even though we both know who the 'hot ass chick' is. My eyes instantly lock onto Allison and right beside her is my sister. I also notice that both of them are dancing very provocatively with two guys I can't stand. My temper flares as I stand up, and Aiden quickly follows. We don't even speak. We know what we need to do to protect the girls. We're both fiercely protective of both of them. Aiden knows I hate Todd and Jason. I'd told him the story freshman year after we played them. We won, of course.

We approach the girls, and Hailey immediately sees us. She stops dancing and flashes a worried glance toward Todd, the dickwad she's dancing with. Allison stops dancing as soon as her eyes find mine.

I'm so angry I want to smash both of their faces in. Todd and Jason went to my rival high school and are total assholes. They're notorious for getting girls drunk out of their mind, using them, and then leaving them alone wherever they happened to be. Rumor has it they raped a girl after their final game senior year, but the girl was so scared, she refused to press charges. Needless to say, they're scum in my book, and now I have to watch my baby sister, who knows how I feel about them, and my girl grinding up on them. Furious isn't a strong enough word to describe the rage running through my veins.

Allison steps away from Jason toward me, and I quickly grab her around the waist and pull her close. Hailey steps forward, like she's going to stop me, and Aiden grabs her and pins her to his side. She's pissed, I can tell, but she has nothing on me. Jason, fuckstick that he is, reaches for Allison, grabbing her arm and pulling.

"What the fuck, MacCoy? Get your hands off my date!" he yells as he tugs on Allison's arm.

"Date?" I look down at Allison with a questioning gaze as she stares wide eyed at Jason and then looks at her arm. I feel her tremble next to me.

"Get your fucking hands off of her, you're hurting her!" I yell at him.

Hailey speaks up, "What the hell, Liam? Why are you going all caveman?"

I grab Jason's wrist and squeeze as tight as I can, so he'll release Allison. Once he drops her hand, I bring it to my chest and cover it with my own to comfort her. I then turn to Hailey. "What are you doing here with them?"

Hailey squares her shoulders and looks me straight in the eye. "Todd and I have been out on a couple of dates."

I pull Allison closer, feeling her start to relax. "What do you mean dates? You're better than this loser."

"Really, Hales?" Aiden asks, his jaw is tense. You can hear the anger in his voice.

Todd has been pretty quiet up to this point; he goes to grab Hailey, but Aiden produces a noise that could only be described as a growl and tucks her in tighter.

"Touch her and die, asshole," Aiden seethes.

"What is wrong with the two of you? We were just dancing!" Hailey shouts.

"Hales, you're dating him?" Aiden asks her, barely able to control his rage.

"No, yes. No. We've been on two dates, this being the second one. GAH!"

"Well, sorry to tell you this one is ending early," I growl.

"Liam! You aren't my ruler. I can date whomever I damn well please," Hailey hisses.

I feel Allison grow tense. I lean down and whisper in her ear, "What about you, sweetheart? Do you want to finish your date?"

Allison meets my gaze, but she doesn't speak, just bites her lip as she turns to look at Jason. "You're coming with me," Jason growls as he reaches for her again. This time he grabs her arm and jerks her toward him.

Allison yells out in pain, or maybe it's fear. Blitzen and the rest of our teammates are at our sides now. I hand Allison off to him. "Watch her!" With that I turn toward Jason and begin to unleash a fury I've never known. I'm faintly aware of Aiden doing the same thing with Todd. I can hear Hailey and Allison yelling for us to stop. I feel a tug on my shoulder, and I look up to see Mike pulling me back. I glance over at Aiden and Scott has his arms behind his back, holding him, as well. I glance down to see Todd and Jason both out cold on the floor. *Serves them right for touching my sister and my girl.*

"I'm good, man," I say, flexing my fist. I can feel my knuckles already starting to swell. Mike releases me, and I make quick work of getting to Allison and wrapping her in my arms. Scott has also released Aiden. Hailey's currently tucked tight against his chest, and he's rubbing her back soothingly. *They're both safe.*

CHAPTER FIFTEEN

Alison

MY HEART IS RACING, Liam and Aiden are throwing blow after blow. Hailey and I are screaming for them to stop. I struggle against Blitzen, yelling at him to let me go. He doesn't, instead he tightens his hold. I look over at one of their teammates, whom I've yet to meet. "Stop them, please!" I cry.

The guy jumps into action and begins pulling on Liam's shoulders. I glance over and there's another one holding Aiden with his arms pinned behind his back. Hailey's standing right beside Aiden, crying and yelling just as hard and loud as I am. The only difference is they don't have her restrained.

Liam stands up and looks at Aiden, who's being released from his hold. Hailey instantly throws her arms around his waist and hugs him tight. Aiden wraps his arms around her, rubbing soothing strokes down her back. Liam moves toward me. He bends his knees to meet my eyes as he lifts my chin with his thumb and forefinger. "You okay, sweetheart?"

I can't help it, I sob harder. Liam mumbles what sounds like, "Fuck", and pulls me close.

Turns out the father of the guy, who was restraining Aiden, owns the place. Scott is the guy's name.

"Hey, guys, you need to leave. I can cover for you," he motions with his head to Todd and Jason, who are now sitting up on the floor, "but you need to leave now."

"Thanks, man," Liam and Aiden say at the same time.

As we walk outside, Liam grabs my hand, and I wince from the tenderness. He stops me by sliding his arm around me. "Allie, baby, what's wrong?" he asks as he wipes the tears from my cheeks.

Aiden and Hailey are at my side. "Ash, what is it?" Aiden questions me.

Liam pulls me to his chest and whispers in my ear, "You're safe. I'm sorry you had to see that."

I sob harder. The sobs are due to the fight I just witnessed, not the pain. Liam assumes otherwise.

Liam looks over at Aiden. "Fuck, man, he was tugging on her trying to get her away from me."

"Ash, we need to take you to get checked out." He's trying to soothe me, keeping his voice calm, but it isn't working.

"Uh, guys, if we all show up at the hospital they're going to get suspicious. Especially since my guess is Todd and Jason both need medical attention. Aiden, you have blood all over your shirt. I don't want you guys getting kicked off the team," Hailey tries to reason.

Liam speaks before anyone else has the opportunity, "I'll take her. Aiden, can you take Hales back to our place? I'll bring Allison back once we're done." He looks down to check to see if he is in the same shape as Aiden. Luckily, he is wearing a black shirt.

"It's nothing. I don't need to go to the hospital," I interrupt them. "He just had a tight grip and it's a little tender, nothing a few Advil won't cure," I try to reason. "I've just never witnessed anything like that before. My emotions are all over the place."

Liam gently pulls my hand to his lips and places a tender kiss on my palm. "Allison, I'm not taking no for an answer. I'd never be able to forgive myself if it turns up broken and I didn't make you get checked." He lowers my hand and wraps his arm around my waist. "Please, let's just let me take you and make sure you're okay," he pleads.

Aiden looks at me for reassurance. "Allison, are you okay with that?" He uses my first name, not my nickname. I know he's trying to make sure I'm comfortable with Liam. I am. He would never hurt me, well, not physically.

I sigh with frustration. "Yes, it's fine. I'll see you guys in a little while. Just know this is not necessary," I tell them.

"Liam." I hear Aiden say, but there's nothing but silence that follows. I look over to see Liam nod his head, then he places his hand on the small of my back to escort me to his SUV.

Liam leads me to his SUV and opens the door. He helps me in the passenger seat, then leans over and buckles my seat belt. He looks up and our faces are mere inches from each other. He brings his hand to my cheek and caresses it with his thumb. "I am so sorry." He kisses me on the forehead, then shuts my door.

As I watch him make his way to the driver's side, I release a frustrated breath. Liam and Aiden are overreacting. My hand doesn't hurt that badly, and I have a feeling the emergency room doctors are going to think I'm vying for attention. Not that I mind Liam taking care of me.

Liam climbs behind the wheel, and then once he has his seat belt on and we're on our way to the emergency room, he reaches over and places his hand on my thigh. The drive is quiet except for the sound of my heart racing. I'm sure Liam can hear it. The minor ache in my hand fades with the feel of Liam caressing my thigh. He goes back and forth from rubbing lazy circles to splaying his long fingers, like he's afraid I'll get away from him. He's driving me insane from just a simple caress.

When we arrive at the emergency room, Liam helps me from the car and wraps his arms around me possessively while he cradles my hand to his chest. We sign in at the reception desk and take a seat in the waiting room. *This is crazy.*

"Let me see," he says softly. He gently picks up my hand and brings it to his lips. He lifts his eyes, meeting with mine. "Baby, I'm so sorry he hurt you." He swallows hard and looks away. "I can't explain what it did to me to see you and Hales being with those two, their hands on you." He turns back to me and his lips meet my forehead. He pulls away and puts his arm around me, pulling me to his chest. I sigh and relax against him.

"Liam, how many times do I have to tell you I'm fine? It's just a little tender. We don't need to be here."

He places his finger over my lips to silence my plea. "Please," he whispers, "for my peace of mind, can we wait for the doctor to see you?"

"Fine," I grumble. I feel him kiss the top of my head as I close my eyes.

I wake up to Liam cradling me in his arms as we walk into an exam bay. He gently lays me down on the table, as he stands beside me, running his fingers through my hair. I open my eyes to look at him. "Hey."

"Hey, you," Liam says as he pulls the chair up next to the bed. He continues to run his fingers through my hair. "The doctor will be in to see you soon. Do you need anything?"

"No, thank you for waiting with me. I'm sure you'd rather be anywhere but here. Sorry." I look away from him. I can feel the tears welling up in my eyes, and I don't want him to see me cry. The frustration with tonight's events are playing havoc with my emotions.

"Hey," he says and I turn to face him. Liam runs his fingers down my cheek, wiping away my tears. "Allie, I would go anywhere with you, there's nowhere else I would rather be."

I would go anywhere with you... What I wouldn't give for those words to be true. The only problem is they are true for me. I want him plain and simple. I know it's wrong to want someone who has a relationship phobia. I'm setting myself up for heartache. Even though

I know the outcome, I can't control it. I refuse to act on it until he's ready to give me more. Deep down I know that will never happen. Liam doesn't think he is capable of more. However, the heart wants what the heart wants, and I'm slowly losing all of mine to Liam MacCoy.

CHAPTER SIXTEEN

Liam

SEEING her tears breaks my heart. She actually thinks I don't want to be here. When I tell her I would go anywhere with her, it's with those words I know I want to chance it. I want it all. I want to be hers and her be mine. She's the one and only person who's ever made me want more than a few hours of sex, more than meaningless. For months I've fought this, and I know sitting here beside her it's not going away. This need I have for her is real.

She focuses her big green eyes on me. "Liam..."

"Shh, baby, let's get you taken care of, we can talk later," I say as I kiss her forehead. As I'm pulling away, the doctor comes into the room.

"Hello, Allison, I'm Dr. Lansing," the doctor says as he sits down on the edge of the bed. "And you are?"

"Liam MacCoy, sir," I say as I reach out and shake his hand.

"Liam MacCoy from UNC?" he questions me.

"Yes, sir, that would be me," I reply with a wink at Allie.

"I'm a big fan, big game next week versus OSU. Season opener."

"Yes, sir."

"Well, then, Miss Hagan, let's get you fixed up. We can't have our star quarterback worrying about his girl; he needs to focus on the big game," he says, grinning at Allison.

"Um, he's—" Allison tries to speak, but I interrupt her. I really like the sound of someone else calling her my girl.

"He's right, baby. Let's get you taken care of, so we can get you home," I tell her.

She looks a little confused, but she smiles at me and nods her head.

After examining Allison, Dr. Lansing states he thinks it is just a bad bruise. He doesn't even ask how it happened. He talks football with me the entire time, except for a few 'does this hurt' questions to Allison. I'm relieved though, because all we need is the media to get wind of this. Dr. Lansing sends Allison for x-rays of her hand, just to be safe. I, of course, refuse to let her go to radiology without me. After about thirty minutes, Dr. Lansing informs us his prediction is correct and the hand is just bruised and swollen. He advises Allison to take Advil as needed for pain and leave the ice pack the nurse gave her on for another thirty minutes.

I help Allison out to the Pathfinder and get her buckled in. She immediately begins to grumble about how she was right and I 'wasted my time' taking her to the emergency room.

I smile. "Thank you, for humoring me. I'll sleep better tonight knowing you really are okay."

"Hmph," is her only reply. She's even sexy when she's mad.

I shoot Aiden and Hales a quick text letting them know she's okay and we're on our way after a quick errand. Looking over to find Allison asleep, I decide to stop at the all-night pharmacy and pick up more Advil. While I'm there, I go ahead and buy a new ice pack and a few other snacks I know she likes. When I return to my Pathfinder, she's still asleep. I find myself constantly sneaking glances at her as I drive us back to my apartment. She's so beautiful. She pulls me in, like a moth to a flame. Smiling at my earlier admission, I'm going to try. I want all of her, and I have never been happier. Convincing her I'm ready might take me a while, but I'm determined, and I never give up on what I want.

I pull up to the apartment and shut the truck off. I lean over and kiss her on the forehead. I hate to wake her up, she looks so peaceful. I grab the bag from the pharmacy and quietly get out of the car. I send Aiden a text telling him to open the door. I make my way to the passenger side, unbuckle her seat belt, and scoop her up in my arms.

"Liam?"

"It's me. We're back at my apartment. Let's get you into bed." Allison mumbles something I can't really make out, but it sounds like 'safe'. I cradle her tight against my chest. *Fuck, this girl has weaved a spell over me.*

"You're safe, baby, I won't let anyone hurt you."

When I reach the door, Aiden's already there, holding it open.

"How is she?" he asks as his eyes take in Allison cradled against my chest.

"She's good. Just bruised and swollen. I stopped at the pharmacy." I motion my head toward the bag I'm holding in my hand for him to take.

"Damn, what all did you get?"

I shrug. "I picked up more Advil, plus an Ace wrap, and an ice pack. I also picked up a few snacks I know she likes." *I've done nothing but watch her since we met.*

Aiden looks at me and smiles. "You're hooked, aren't you?"

"More than you know, my man, more than you know." I continue down the hall and stop at my bedroom door.

"Liam, Hales is already in there asleep. After we got your text she was wiped out, so I convinced her to go on to bed. I had to promise if anything changed, I would wake her up."

Fuck! I want Allison in my bed. I want to take care of her. I turn and headed back toward the living room; she can sleep on the couch, and I'll take the chair.

"Um, Liam, Blitzen is here, remember?" Aiden smirks. He knows this is killing me, and he's enjoying the hell out of it.

"Fine," I mumble as I walk into his bedroom. I lay Allison down on the bed. As I do, she reaches for me.

"Liam."

"Shh. You're in Aiden's room," I tell her.

"Here," Aiden says, handing her a shirt of his to sleep in.

I glare at Aiden, and he smirks at me, yet again. He knows what it does to me to have her in his clothes. He knows I want her in my bed with me. *Asshole.*

Allison starts to sit up. "Let me help you." I lean down and place my arm around her back and gently lift her, so she's sitting on the side of the bed.

She looks up at me with a small grin. "Are you going to help me change?" My heart stops. This beautiful amazingly sexy creature is looking at me with innocent, trusting eyes, asking me to help her remove her clothes for bed. Before I can get my brain to function, so I can respond, Aiden is protesting.

"Ash, I can go get Hales. She just laid down, I'm sure she wouldn't mind helping you," Aiden suggests.

Allison looks at Aiden like he's crazy. "Why would I wake her when Liam can help me?" she says it so matter of fact, like me undressing her is as normal as breathing. My stalled heart is now thundering in my chest. It's beating so loud, I'm sure they can both hear it. Somehow, I'm able to make myself speak above the thunder inside my chest. I cup her cheek in the palm of my hand. "I can get Hales if that would make you feel more comfortable." *Please, say you still want me to do it.* Hell yes, I'm being selfish, but my protective instincts are in overdrive when it comes to Allison. I'll always want it to be me.

Allison smiles up at me before turning her gaze on Aiden. "Can you give us a few minutes, so I can change?"

Aiden gives me a warning look before nodding his head and backing out of the room. I know he's worried I'll hurt her, but what he doesn't realize is I could never, would never. I'll protect her with everything in me. I stand here staring into her green eyes and I'm overcome with emotion. I'm going to do it. I'm going all in with this girl, and I'm excited at the concept. There are no doubts floating through my mind. I crave her unlike anything I've never known. Suddenly, I need to make it real. I need her to tell me that it's me. That no other man will ever touch her again, because the next time I'm not so sure I'll be able to stop until I kill the fucker.

I drop to my knees in front of her, so we're eye to eye. She raises her eyebrow at me in question. I place my hands on both of her cheeks before leaning in and placing a kiss on her forehead. "Allison, I know you said you want more, that you want it all." I swallow the lump in my throat. Just because I'm positive this is what I want doesn't mean I'm not scared as hell that I still won't be enough for her, be what she wants. I take a deep breath and continue. "I want you, all of you. I never want to go through what I went through tonight ever again. When I saw his hands on you…" I shake my head to attempt to erase the memory. I gently pick up her hand and cradle it against my chest, right above my heart. Her eyes soften, and I know she can feel the thunderous rhythm playing inside me. Gently I kiss her hand. "I want to be with you, only you. I want to be the one who holds you at night, the one who gets your kisses and your smiles." I brush my fingers across her cheek.

I feel her hand tremble against my chest. She's just as affected by me as I am by her. "Liam, you know I don't want casual. I don't expect you to propose, but you told me yourself, you don't want a serious relationship. How can I be sure you've really changed your mind?" She places her soft hand against my cheek. "I feel such a connection with you, it would only be a matter of time before I fall head over heels. You would have the power to break me, break my heart. I'm not sure I can take that chance."

"Baby, I'm taking a chance too. I've never felt this way about anyone. Never has my entire world been turned upside down because of a beautiful girl consuming my every thought, every emotion." I take a deep breath, this is it; I'm going to let this girl in. I'm giving her the power to destroy me. "I'm taking a chance too, beautiful girl, but you have to take one on me as well. We'll be in this together, you and me. You're all that matters," I whisper as I crush my mouth to hers. I need to taste her. I need her to understand this isn't a game, not just a hookup. She is mine—I want her to be mine, need her to be mine.

CHAPTER SEVENTEEN

Allison

I'M TRYING to process what Liam just said. He tells me I'm all that matters, and then he crushes his mouth to mine. I moan deep in my throat. I can't control it, even if I wanted to. The taste of his lips on mine is annihilating my common sense. I don't want to fight this anymore. I want him and his kisses. I reach up and wrap my arms around his neck, pulling him in as close as I can get him. He drags his lips away, and I groan at the loss. He continues his assault on my senses by placing kisses on my cheek, down my neck. He pulls away, breathing heavy, as his hands make their way to the hem of my shirt. Without question or thought, I raise my arms in the air. Liam gently raises my shirt over my head. He then takes my hand and helps me stand. I watch as he places kisses on my collarbone, down my chest, working his way down my stomach. Once he reaches the waist of my jeans, he looks up at me with hooded eyes, seeking my approval. I can only nod my head as I run my hands through his hair. Liam slowly unbuttons my jeans and slides them down as he peppers kisses on my thighs.

Once my jeans hit my ankles, I step out of them with Liam's assistance. He stands and wraps his right arm around my waist while placing his left hand behind my neck to pull me close to him. He crashes his lips to mine and kisses me with so much passion that if he wasn't holding onto me, I would fall to the floor in a puddle of lust. I never want him to stop. I want to spend every second of every day wrapped in his arms being consumed by his kisses.

Suddenly, there's a knock at the door. "Ash, you guys done in there?" Aiden yells through the door.

Liam pulls away and places his forehead against mine. "He has impeccable timing. You might want to answer him, baby. I don't think he would trust me if I said you were fine."

"Give us a minute, Ace!" I yell back. How I'm able to find my voice and use it is beyond me. What started out as me flirting with Liam, asking him to help me change, turned into confessions and scorching kisses. I'm perfectly capable of changing on my own, my hand doesn't even hurt. *What has gotten into me?*

"What are we doing, Liam? What does this mean?"

Liam stares at me intently. "I would like to think I was kissing my girlfriend while helping her change," he sheepishly replies.

"Girlfriend?" I whisper.

"Girlfriend," he whispers back in confirmation.

I try to control my emotions at this sexy man calling me his girlfriend. I'm also trying really hard not to let my insecurities consume me. I just had my first kiss a few months ago and now here I stand in nothing but my underwear with Liam's sexy body wrapped around me, and he's calling me his girlfriend. *Holy Shit!* I should be nervous being exposed to him, my first time ever being exposed to a guy. However, I'm not nervous. Liam makes me feel safe, protected, wanted.

I take a deep breath. I'm tired of fighting it. I'm going to take a chance on Liam, just like he asked me to. I just hope my heart can take it when he walks away and realizes I'm not what he wants after all. I take another deep breath. "Well, I guess you better help your girlfriend get changed before Aiden starts beating down the door."

The smile that lights up Liam's face is one I've never seen before. He kisses me tenderly, then engulfs me in his big strong arms for the greatest hug I've ever received. "You're really mine?" he asks me, pulling back only far enough to look into my eyes.

I nod. I'm not capable of more than that, my emotions are running rampant.

Liam pulls away and takes his dress shirt off. He pulls the t-shirt he has on underneath it off, and has it over my head before I know what's happening. He shrugs back into his dress shirt and buttons it up. "I can't have my girl sleeping in another man's shirt, now can I? It's bad enough you're sleeping in his bed." He takes a deep breath. "I know he's like a brother to you, but I want you next to me, wrapped in my arms. I want you to be the last thing I see before I fall asleep and the first thing I see when I wake up," he says as he kisses below my ear, trailing down my neck. I feel him slip his hands under the t-shirt and caress my back. The next thing I know, he has my bra unhooked and is helping me pull it through my sleeves.

"Tonight is the last night you'll ever sleep in another man's bed. I'm going out tomorrow and buying a futon, so if Blitzen is here there will still be enough places to sleep for Hales, him, and Aiden. Because you, my beautiful girlfriend, will be in my bed with me." He then picks up all of my discarded clothes, places a kiss on my temple, and says he'll be right back as he leaves the room with my clothes.

I can hear him talking to Aiden in the hallway. He tells Aiden he needs to get me something really quick before Aiden can come back in. Well, actually what he really says is, "Don't fucking go in there, I'll be right back, she's not decent, yet." I don't hear Aiden's reply.

Liam comes rushing back into the room, holding a pair of sweatpants. "I know these will swallow you, but I can't stand the thought of you sleeping in just a t-shirt in his bed." He looks almost embarrassed at his admission.

I roll my eyes at him as he drops to my feet and begins dressing me in his sweats. He gently pulls me off the bed to pull them up over my hips. "Let's get you tucked in, so we can get this night over with and get you back in my arms where you belong."

I slide under the covers as Liam bends down to kiss me goodnight. "Goodnight, my beautiful girlfriend," he whispers, then turns and walks toward the door.

"Liam," I call out to him.

He turns to look at me. "Yeah, baby?"

"What did you do with my clothes?"

He smiles his panty melting smile. "I put them in my room where they belong." He winks, then turns and opens the door. "Keep your fucking hands off my girl, Emerson." I hear him tell Aiden as he passes him in the hall.

Aiden enters the room shaking his head. "What was that about?" he asks me.

I smile. "He brought me a pair of sweats to sleep in," I say, shrugging my shoulders.

Aiden picks up his shirt lying on the chair. "I see he found you a different shirt to sleep in as well."

"Yes, he's having a hard enough time with his girlfriend sleeping in another man's bed, the clothes he could easily fix," I say, like I hadn't just announced news I was sure would affect all four of our lives in some aspect.

Aiden's mouth drops open in shock, but he's able to quickly recover. "Did you just call yourself Liam MacCoy's girlfriend?" he questions me, like I've lost my ever lovin' mind.

I smile again. I'm unable to prevent it. I'm happy. "I did," confirming he heard me correctly.

"Would you mind elaborating on that subject for me?"

I sigh. "Liam and I have been tiptoeing around our attraction for one another since the day we met. He knew I wanted more, but he wasn't sure he could give me what I wanted. Now he says he can. I'm taking a chance on him." I pause to gauge his reaction. "We're taking a chance on each other."

Aiden's quiet for several minutes while he processes what I just said. "Is this what you want? Are you happy?"

"Yes, and yes I am. There's this connection between us, Ace. I can't explain it, but I want him, and I'm willing to risk a broken heart to have him."

Aiden nods in understanding before I'm even finished speaking. "Liam's a great guy, my best friend, aside from you. If anything, Liam is a man of his word. He would never lead you astray on purpose. Not to mention, he's never had a girlfriend. I've watched him mope around here, since the day he met you. I've seen him turn other girls away, saying he would just be pretending they were you." He smiles at me. "I've lectured and warned him off of you. Threatening if he starts anything, he'd better be serious. We've been thick as thieves, since freshman year, and I've never seen him act like this. He really is into you."

Again with the smiling. My face is going to be sore tomorrow. "I want to see where this goes. I feel safe with him, wanted-" I don't bother to elaborate; Aiden knows how I feel about being alone in the world. "Shit."

"What is it, what's wrong?" Aiden asks, concern lacing his voice.

"I'm Liam MacCoy's girlfriend," I whisper.

Aiden throws his head back and laughs.

"It's not funny. I'm in your bed, sleeping next to you, while my very new, very sexy boyfriend is sleeping just down the hall." I can see why Liam is so frustrated. I'm not so sure I could handle him sleeping with another girl, best friend and adopted sister or not. He really is practicing great restraint with this entire situation. I'll need to make sure I make it up to him.

"It's not your fault, and, besides, with you and Liam being an official couple this will not happen again. Liam will make sure of that." Laughing, Aiden leans over and kisses my cheek. "Night, Ash."

"Night, Ace."

CHAPTER EIGHTEEN

Liam

IT TAKES all the fucking willpower I have to walk away from Allison. She's all snuggled up under the covers in fucking Aiden's bed. *Jackass.* In reality, I know it has nothing to do with Aiden and it's simply the bad luck of Blitzen being flooded out of his apartment, as well as me not wanting to make Hales sleep with Aiden. I'm hoping she'll ask me to do just that. I won't be able to tell her no. Unfortunately, that doesn't happen.

I make it to my room, and Hales is sound asleep. I change into gym shorts and climb in beside her. I love my little sister, we're close, but I don't really like her all that much at the moment. *I'm definitely getting a futon tomorrow.* Little sis and I are going to have a long chat tomorrow about her choice of dates; Todd and Jason of all people to go on a date with. *What the fuck was she thinking?* Either one of them could have been hurt worse than Allison's bruised hand. The thought of either one of them hurt in any way has me seeing red. After what seems like hours, I finally fall asleep.

I wake to the sound of footsteps in the hallway. I immediately open my eyes and hop out of bed. Today is a new day, and I'm going to spend every damn minute of it with my girlfriend. I stall, waiting for the panic to set in—nothing.

I make my way down the hall, following the noise, which leads me to the kitchen. I find Allison standing at the sink, opening the new bottle of Advil I bought last night. I stand here just watching her. She's so sexy, even in my sweats that swallow her, and she's all mine. *Finally.* She must sense me watching her because she looks up. "Good morning, beautiful," I say as I make quick work of the space between us. I pull her back against my chest and nuzzle her neck. "Need some help?"

She exhales. "Yes, please." She hands me the bottle, and I reluctantly let her go to open it for her. "I can never get these damn things open."

"How are you feeling today?"

Allison shrugs her shoulders. "I'm fine, Liam. I have more of a headache than anything."

I lead her to the table and pull out a chair for her. "Sit while I make you some coffee. You probably need to eat something with this as well, eggs and toast okay?" I ask her as I shuffle about the kitchen, making coffee and grabbing eggs out of the fridge.

"Thank you, but I can just grab a Pop-Tart or something back at the dorm. You don't need to wait on me."

I immediately stop what I'm doing and stalk to the table and kneel down in front of her. I tuck a loose piece of her hair, which has fallen out of its holder, behind her ear. "First of all, I know I don't have to make you breakfast, I want to. Second, you need to get used to me taking care of you. You're my girl." I kiss her on the forehead. "And third, why are you going back to the dorm so early? I thought maybe we could hang out today." I rise to my feet and go back to making breakfast.

"I need to get clean clothes and call Gran to check on her." She pauses. "Besides, I wasn't sure you wanted me to stick around. I thought maybe you might have regrets about the whole girlfriend thing." She averts her gaze, looking at the wall in front of her.

As soon as I hear the word regret out of her mouth, I panic. I'm at her chair in three strides. I bend down, scoop her up, then sit in her chair, placing her on my lap. I wrap one arm around her, holding her tight against me while the other rubs circles on her thigh. "Allie, look at me." I wait patiently. Internally I'm unnerved waiting until she turns to face me. "I cannot, and will not, ever regret you. I'm all in. You and I are taking a chance on each other, remember?" She nods her head in agreement and it suddenly hits me—maybe she's the one with regrets. I take a deep breath "Unless, do you ...." I can barely get the question out before I start to get flustered. I just got her, I can't lose her. "So—do you regret your decision to take a chance on us?" I whisper, too afraid of what she might say.

"What? No, of course not. I thought, maybe in the light of day, you would, you know, maybe change your mind about me, about us."

Instead of responding, I pull her close and kiss her. I start out slow and easy, but when she parts her lips and invites me in, I take full advantage. I thrust my tongue into her mouth, gently caressing her thighs with my hands. The taste of her on my tongue is amazing. *Will I ever get enough?* Allison pulls away, and I groan in protest. She meets my gaze and licks her lips as she stands up then sits back down, straddling my hips. *Hell yes.* I envelope her body in my arms, and she resumes her sensual assault on my mouth. Allison places her hands on my shoulders and rocks her hips into my erection. I moan deep in my throat. Before I know what's happening, Allison pulls away and buries her head between my neck and shoulder. Confused from the lust coursing through my body, it takes me a few seconds to realize what's happening. Hales, Aiden, and Blitzen are all three standing in the kitchen doorway beside us, mouths gaping.

I smile over at my sister and my two best friends as I rub circles on Allison's back. She keeps her head buried in my neck, and I'm just fine with that. I cherish the fact that I'm the one holding her close. "Good morning," I address them. That seems to snap them out of their stupor, and they pile into the kitchen. Hales takes over making breakfast, Aiden makes coffee, and Blitzen sits at the island, just taking it all in. Continuing to rub my hands up and down her back, I pull Allison just far enough away, so I can look in her eyes. "You okay, baby?"

She nods her head yes. Her face is still flushed from embarrassment. Without thinking, I lift her in my arms, and she instinctively wraps her legs around my waist and clasps her arms tight around my neck. I feel the grin spread across my face as I carry her down the hall to my bedroom. I kick the door closed with my foot. I walk over to the bed and sit down. Allison remains wrapped around me, no sign of moving, so I scoot back on the bed and lie down, and she stretches out beside me, her legs entangled with mine. I gently brush the hair out of her eyes. "You okay, beautiful girl?"

She offers me a small smile. "Yeah. This is all just so new to me."

Fuck. "I'm sorry, I let myself get out of control, but you tasted amazing. I promise I'll never force you to do anything you aren't ready for."

"No, it's not you, Liam. I liked what we were doing. I'm the one who straddled you, remember?"

I laugh. "How could I forget?" I say as I run my hands over her hips. "So, what is it then?"

I can see the blush rising across her face. "I guess I'm just embarrassed we got caught. I'm not sure how we do this. I mean, I know you called me your girlfriend, but are you okay with what just happened in there? Are you okay that they caught us?" She nervously chews on her bottom lip as she focuses on the ceiling. "Is it okay if people see us like that?" This last question is almost a whisper.

I'm dumbfounded. This beautiful, smart, incredibly sexy girl thinks I want to keep her a secret. Did she not hear me last night when I told her I was all in? Hell yes, I want people to see, especially all of those fuckers who watch her every move. *She's mine, damn it.* She's staring at the ceiling so I sit up on my elbow, I'm now looking down at her. I have her full attention. "Allison, you and I are together now. You agreed to be my girlfriend, and I refuse to let you take it back." I kiss her nose. "I want the entire world to know we're together. I want you, all of you, and the more people who know you're mine, the better. So, to answer your questions—no, I'm not embarrassed, and hell yes, I want them to see us." With that I kiss her hard. She immediately opens her mouth for me, and my tongue finds its way into her warmth. Allison moans deep in her throat, and if I wasn't already harder than a rock, I would've been in this moment. I find myself on top of her, bracing my weight with my hands on either side of her head. Her legs fall open and invite me in. Even though she is wearing sweats, and even through my shorts, I can feel her heat.

Somehow, I'm able to see through the hunger I have for her to realize we're in a compromising position. I want things with Allison to be perfect. Her first time needs to be special. I slowly end the kiss and drop my head to her chest. "We need to stop, before I'm not able to."

Allison lifts her hips into mine. "What if I don't want to stop?"

Holy shit, she's trying to kill me. "I want nothing more than to bury myself deep inside of you and never leave. What I don't want is my sister and two best friends in the next room. I want our first time together to be special." I roll off the bed and stand up, pulling her up with me. I draw her into a hug so tight I'm probably cutting off her air supply. I can't get her close enough. "You're special, Allison. You're not just some girl. I need to prove to you how important you are to me."

She places her hand on the back of my neck and pulls my lips back to hers. I gently run my tongue along her bottom lip before biting down gently. She moans, and I know I need to slow down, so I kiss her lips softly one more time before pulling back. *Fuck, I don't want to stop kissing her.*

I cradle her cheeks. "I want nothing more than to stay here in this bed with you all day, but we need to go shopping." I place one more chaste kiss on her lips and pull away. "Now, let's get you some break-fast. You have a phone call to make before we head out."

CHAPTER NINETEEN

Allison

I'M MORTIFIED when everyone walks in on me grinding on Liam. What the hell has gotten into me? I have my first official boyfriend for less than twenty-four hours and I turn into a slut. *Ugh!* I know slut is pushing it, but that's exactly what I feel like when they walk in on us. Then I realize Liam might not want them seeing us like this and my embarrassment rises even more. I can feel the heat in my face, so I keep it buried in Liam's neck. Not that I'm complaining about that part.

Liam carries me to his room and cuddles with me. Yes, my six-foot-four boyfriend is a big teddy bear. He reassures me he wants me, and he wants the entire world to know it. I must admit, I melt when he says that. It's hard to think that out of all the girls he's been with he would choose me to actually have a commitment with. I'm still stunned.

I let Liam lead the way back out to the kitchen where Hailey, Aiden, and Blitzen are sitting at the table eating breakfast. I can feel my face getting hot as we walk into the room. Liam pulls out the remaining chair and plops down, as he pulls me down onto his lap. Blitzen winks at me, and Aiden laughs out loud. Jackass, he knows I'm embarrassed. My dear roommate, Hailey, Liam's little sister, goes straight for the kill.

"Holy shit, that was hot! I'm never going to bed early again," she says as she sips her coffee. "I always miss the good stuff."

And there it is, my good friend embarrassment. Front and center. Liam chuckles as he places his hand on my belly and pulls me back against him.

"Hales, Blitzen, Aiden," he waits until he has their attention, "I would like to introduce you to my girlfriend, Allison." He beams. Yes, my badass quarterback boyfriend is beaming at his admission that I am indeed his girlfriend. The pride and admission in his statement causes a burning deep inside me.

None of them respond with anything other than a smile. After what they just saw, I don't think words are necessary.

Liam starts making a plate of bacon, eggs, and toast, then places it in front of me. Hailey sees he isn't about to let me go and brings us both a cup of coffee and orange juice. I just stare at the plate, still in a daze from everything that has transpired since I woke up this morning. Liam notices I'm not eating. "You want me to make you something else?" he whispers in my ear, which causes goose bumps to cover my entire body.

I shake my head and pick up my fork and start to eat. It isn't until I look up and see all three of them watching us that I realize Liam and I aren't only eating off the same plate, we're even feeding each other. He offers me bites, and I'm doing the same. He still has one arm wrapped tight around me with his fingers splayed over my belly. Needless to say, it's hard to concentrate on eating. I think that's why I started feeding him as well, I needed the distraction.

Liam following my gaze, looks up to see everyone watching us. "What?"

The only response we get is laughter, throw your head back, tears streaming laughter. Before long, Liam and I are laughing right along with them. After breakfast we all pitch in to help clean up.

Once we're done, Liam drives Hales and me back to The Warehouse to get her car. "So, I'll see you in an hour?" he asks me as he draws me in for a hug. I can't help but notice we're a perfect fit as I tuck my head under his chin. *Liam gives the best hugs.*

I look over at Hailey. "What are your plans for the day?"

"I'm meeting some friends from high school for lunch, and then after that I got nothing."

"So, can I pick you up at the dorm in an hour? I want to go shopping for a futon, and I thought we could just hang out, spend the day together?" Liam asks me. I had forgotten he said he was buying a futon.

"What the hell do you need a futon for?" Hailey asks him.

Liam smiles down at me. "Well, my little sister tends to spend the night a lot and so does my buddy Blitzen. In the past this hasn't been an issue. However, things have changed; my girlfriend will be placing a permanent reservation on sharing my bed with me whenever she would like, so I need to ensure my little sister has a comfortable place to sleep, which does not include being curled up with either of my male best friends." He says the last part with tension in his voice, like he can picture Hailey curled up with Aiden or Blitzen.

Hailey grins. When I say grins, we're talking face-splitting blind you kind of grin. "You fell hard, huh, big brother?" Then she turns to me. "Can't wait for my spa day."

Liam kisses my forehead. "And still falling." His simple statement seems to make sense to Hailey as she nods her head.

"Alright, future sister-in-law, get your ass in the car, so my brother can go shopping for his futon." Hailey winks at Liam.

Liam leans down and kisses me soft, sweet, and slow. "See you in an hour, beautiful girl." Her statement doesn't seem to bother him in the least.

As soon as we're in the car and driving away from Liam, Hailey is all over me. "Holy fucking shit, what in the hell did you do to my brother?"

I turn in my seat and gape at her. "Umm, I'm not sure what you mean?"

"What I mean is I've never, in my entire existence, seen him act all sweet and loving with a girl. I've never seen him show any public displays of affection. Hell, he was cuddling, and you two were feeding each other at the damn breakfast table."

"Oh, that. Well, I'm not sure, I don't know how Liam was with other girls, so I can't say. I know what you've told me, and what Aiden and Liam, himself, has told me." I shrug, like it's no big deal.

"Allow me to enlighten you, my friend. Liam does not do PDA. Ever. He picks a girl up at a party, the bar, what have you, they do their thing and it's done. No affection whatsoever. Never has he claimed a girlfriend and never has he practically begged a girl to spend time with him, like he did back there. You, my friend, have tamed the beast."

I can't help it, I laugh out loud to that one. "Tamed the beast, really, Hales?"

She nods. "Yes, the beast. Just wait, if he continues this way, you'll hear that a lot."

I really can't comment, because I have no idea why Liam chose me over all the other girls he has been with or could be with. I just hope he doesn't break my heart because one thing is for sure; I'm falling hard for Liam MacCoy, and he has the power to crush me.

Once we arrive back at the dorm, I call Gran. I tell her I've met an amazing guy, who's my roommate's brother, and he asked me on a date tonight. She understands, of course, and wants to hear all about Liam. I refrain from telling her that he is 'officially' my boyfriend. I don't know why, but I want to keep that just for me, for the time being.

After talking to Gran longer than time allowed, I rush through a shower. I throw on a green sun dress, which Hailey says makes my eyes pop, and a pair of matching flip-flops. I braid my hair off to the side, add some mascara and lip gloss, and I'm good to go. Just as I'm unplugging my phone from its charger, there's a knock at the door.

"Come in!" I yell. I know it's Liam. I'm not expecting anyone else.

Liam walks through the door with a frown on his face. Great, it's only been an hour and he's changed his mind. Stay calm, don't let him see you cry.

"Hey, you." I try to sound as cheerful as I can.

"Why wasn't your door locked, and why did you just yell for me to come in? I could have been anyone." He scowls.

I wrap my arms around his waist and rest my head, in what I like to think of as my spot, right below his chin. His arms immediately crush me to him. "I knew you were going to be here any minute, and Hales just left; she must have forgotten to lock it on her way out."

Liam kisses my temple. "I don't want anything to happen to you or my little sister. You guys need to make sure you keep this locked, even during the day, and always make sure you know who's at the door."

I nod my head in agreement, trying hard not to smile. It's been a long damn time since anyone other than Gran or Aiden and his family has worried about me. I'm overcome with emotion and afraid if I try to speak Liam will see, and I'm not ready to go there with him just yet. So, I lean up on my tiptoes and kiss him long and hard.

"You look beautiful," he says as he pulls away. "You ready to go?"

"Yes." I grab my phone and my wristlet.

"Where's your bag?"

"Oh, I'm just going to take this," I say, showing him my wristlet. "It can carry everything I'll need, including my phone."

Liam looks at the floor. "I thought you were going to stay with me."

"Oh." I knew we're shopping for a bed, but I didn't realize that meant I was staying there tonight. "You want me to stay with you tonight?"

"Every night, beautiful girl, but I'll take what I can get. It's just

..." Liam rubs his hand on the back of his neck. "I really just want to fall asleep with you in my arms and wake up the same way. I promise nothing else will happen, I just want that, with you. Last night, I laid awake in bed, knowing you were sleeping next to Aiden. I need you with me tonight."

Wow. "Okay, let me pack a few things." I rush around grabbing clean underwear, a pair of shorts, and a tank. I throw in my cell charger, as well as my bathroom necessities. When I'm ready to leave, Liam's by my side, taking my tote out of my hands, throwing it over his shoulder. He locks the door to my dorm, laces his fingers through mine, and we're on our way.

The day is amazing. Liam buys the first futon he sees at the furniture store and arranges for delivery today at four. He claims when he tells his parents it's for Hailey they won't blink at the credit card statement. He calls Aiden to make sure he's going to be home to accept the delivery. We go to Walmart and buy a new futon cover along with extra blankets and pillows. Liam insisted I pick up my brand of shampoo and body wash to keep at his place, as well as my own loofa. We also pick up some groceries and a few items Aiden asked us to pick up. We grab Subway for lunch and eat it at the park.

Throughout the day, Liam's constantly touching me. Holding my hand, his arm over my shoulder, hands on my hips when he's standing behind me, hand on the small of my back, leading me through doorways. I'm on sensory overload.

When we arrive at his apartment, he calls Aiden to help carry in the loot. I, of course, am not allowed to help. I am, however, allowed to hold the door open and supervise. *Ugh.* He needs to realize I've been taking care of myself and Gran for a long time. When I tell him so he says that *'it's his privilege to take care of me now.'* I have no response to that.

"What the hell did you guys buy?" Aiden asks us as he and Liam set the last of the bags on the kitchen counter.

"Just some food and new blankets and pillows for the futon, and I had Allie pick up the shampoo and body wash she likes for when she stays here. This way she doesn't have to pack it each time or rush home." He winks in my direction.

"I see," is all Aiden says in reply. It's obvious he's having a hard time adjusting to my relationship with Liam, unlike Hailey, she's thrilled. "By the way, what's with the futon purchase?" he asks, motioning to the living room where the recently delivered futon is set up in the corner.

Liam shrugs. "Hales and Blitzen spend the night a lot, and now Allie does too," he says as he's pressing his front to my back and wrapping his arms around my waist. "I wanted to make sure everyone has a comfortable place to sleep, preferably without my little sister being shacked up with you or Blitzen."

I can tell Aiden is goading Liam by the look in his eyes "What's wrong with how we've been doing things? Allison with me, Hales with you, and Blitzen on the couch?" I can see the effort it's taking him not to laugh.

Liam growls. "Allison will be sleeping with me, in my bed from now on. There will be no exceptions. The futon is for Hales. Blitzen and whoever else can fight over the couch, but Allison will be with me."

Aiden throws his head back and roars with laughter. It takes him a few minutes to get himself under control while Liam glares at him. I stand here with a smile on my face only Aiden can see. Liam grabs our personal supplies and pulls me into his bedroom and shuts the door. He drops my tote on the bed. "The top two drawers are yours. I cleaned them out this morning when I got back. If you need more space, let me know." He places a kiss on my temple and carries the rest of our supplies to his adjacent bathroom. And here I stand with a silly grin on my face.

CHAPTER TWENTY

Liam

WHEN I COME out of the bathroom, Allison is still standing in the same spot. "What's wrong, babe?"

"You made room for my stuff in your dresser?" she asks me, like it's the craziest thing she's ever heard.

Everyone seems to be really shocked with me the last few weeks. I've never wanted a girlfriend before Allison. It wasn't necessarily because I was against it, no girl had ever held my attention long enough to want to try, until Allison. All I could see was football. It's only been less than twenty-four hours since she agreed to be with me and instead of the panic I was afraid would set in, it's excitement. I rushed home after dropping her off and immediately cleared out my top two dresser drawers for her. I then cleaned out a drawer in the bathroom, as well as a shelf in the bathroom closet. The thought of her spending that much time here with me brings a smile to my face. The only other thing that's ever done that is football.

"Yeah, I also have a drawer and a shelf for you in the bathroom, that's where I put all of your toiletry stuff." By this time, I'm standing beside her, and I lift her chin with my forefinger, so she's looking me in the eye. "I want you, I want you here. This is all new to me, these feelings and this need I have for you. Just knowing your stuff is mixed with mine makes me happy. I'm going to give this everything I have, Allison." I kiss her nose and walk away because if I don't I'll have her under me on my bed in no time flat.

"So, what do you want to do tonight?" I ask as I sit down on the bed. Before Allison can respond, there's a knock on my bedroom door and Aiden pops his head in.

"Dude, what the fuck? What if Allison would have been changing or something? You can't just walk in without permission anymore, man," I growl at him.

Aiden just chuckles. "Chill out, I'll wait for an invitation in the future."

"Damn right, you will."

"Anyway," he rolls his eyes, "I just wanted to let you guys know Blitzen and a few of the guys are coming over later to play cards and watch movies."

Allison steps between my legs and places her arms around my neck. My hands instantly reach for her hips. "I guess we have our answer." She smiles down at me. *My girl is beautiful.*

I shake my head. "We can do anything you want. We don't have to stay here, or we can just lock ourselves in my room. I don't care either way, just as long as you're close to me."

Aiden clears his throat behind us. "All righty then. I'll let you two get back to what you were doing. Oh, and, Ash, I talked to Mom, and she spent the afternoon with Gran. She said Gran's doing well." He winks at us and leaves the room.

I rest my forehead on her belly as she runs her hands through my hair. "Liam, really, we can do whatever you want. I just want to spend time with you. These last twenty-four hours have been amazing, and I'm not ready for it to end yet."

I tug her down on my lap and tuck her hair behind her ear. "Baby,

I don't want this to end either. I fought my attraction for you. No, attraction isn't the right word, more like longing. I fought this longing I've had for you since the day we met. When I said that I wanted to take a chance and be in this relationship with you, I meant it," I pause to kiss her, "but now that I've had this time with you, with you being mine, and us being together like we have," I kiss her again, I just can't help myself, "I never want it to end. It's not even been twenty-four hours and I know it's only you." She kisses me.

Allison backs away from our kiss, stands up, and walks to the door. I start to panic that I've scared her away, but when I see her push the door shut and turn the lock, I know she feels the same way. I scoot back against the headboard, hoping she'll curl up beside me, so I can hold her. *Never had those thoughts before, MacCoy.*

My beautiful girlfriend has other plans. She climbs up on the bed and straddles my hips, crushing her mouth to mine. Once again, the taste and feel of her consumes my senses. She opens her mouth and my tongue meets hers stroke for stroke. She places her hands on my shoulders and begins to rock back and forth against my erection. She's slow, and hesitant at first. A few minutes in I can tell she's feeling it, and starting to let go. I can feel her heat through our clothes, clothes I'm currently cursing and blessing at the same time. I don't want to rush her, but I would give anything to be inside of her. *I'm a fucking mess.*

"Liam," she moans against my lips, and my hands instantly brace her hips, assisting her with her release. I want to give this to her, giving her pleasure is all that matters. I know that she's new to all of this, so we need to take our time. However, this I can give her. Allison moans and breaks away from our kiss. I can tell she's getting close, and so am I. Watching my beautiful girl bring herself to orgasm by simply kissing me and rocking her hips against mine, is making me feel like a thirteen-year-old boy again.

"Let go, baby." I continue to guide her hips back and forth over my erection. Fuck, I'm not sure I'm going to last much longer.

Allison arches her back, and I can feel her body shudder, just as I throw my head back with her name on my lips. I reach for her and draw her close to me, crushing her chest to mine as I kiss the top of her head.

Allison is quiet and still in my arms. After several minutes of silence, I hear her soft voice. "I'm sorry."

What? "Sorry for what, baby?" I have no idea what she's apologizing for; she's responsible for the hottest, most erotic event in my life, and she's apologizing.

"For that, I shouldn't have attacked you like I did. It's just you were being so sweet and well, I wanted to be as close to you as possible."

"Allie." I wait for her to look at me, but she doesn't. "Allie, baby, look at me please." She slowly sits up on the bed and meets my gaze. "You're not allowed to be sorry for what we did. What we just did was hot and sexy, and hot." I clasp her face with both hands. "You're beautiful, sexy, amazing, and mine. You make me feel things I've never felt, and it's euphoric, almost as much as the orgasm you just gave me." I wink at her.

"Did—did you?" She blushes at the words she's trying to say.

"Yes, beautiful girl, I just got off in my pants because my sexy as fuck girlfriend was driving me crazy." I laugh "You're turning me back into my thirteen-year-old self," I voice my earlier thoughts.

She giggles, and it's the most beautiful sound I've ever heard. I kiss her partly because I can't keep my hands off her and partly because I can. She's mine, and I don't have to fight these feelings anymore. I'm starting to get uncomfortable with the mess in my pants; I'm certain she has the same problem.

"Allison, do you trust me?" I ask as I draw myself away from her lips.

She nods. "Yes, Liam, I trust you."

"Well, I need to clean up, and I'm sure you do too. I thought maybe you could take a shower with me? I promise I'll be good, I just…"

"Yes," she replies as she tugs me off the bed. There is not a single ounce of hesitation in her voice. The trust she's giving me is humbling.

Stunned, I'm stunned. Yeah, I asked her, and I wanted her to say yes, but in reality, I knew, well, I thought I knew, her saying yes was a long shot. I let Allison lead me to the bathroom. I can feel her hand trembling in mine.

"Allie, you don't have to do this. I'm sorry, I shouldn't have asked." I brush my thumb over her knuckles, trying to soothe her.

"I trust you, Liam. I don't feel pressured. I'm just nervous and worried, I guess."

I pick her up and set her on the counter. "What's going on in that head of yours?" I step between her legs and run my hands up and down her arms.

"I've never been naked in front of a guy before, or anyone really, not since I was a little girl. What if I disappoint you?"

"Allie, you are the most beautiful girl I've ever seen. There's no way you could ever disappoint me." I kiss her neck right below her ear. "Let me show you how beautiful you are?"

She raises her hands above her head, and I slowly lift her dress and remove it from her body. I have to swallow the emotion in my throat. She's perfect, the most perfect creature I've ever seen. I almost didn't have this moment, almost lost the opportunity to be here with her like this, to show her how amazing and special she is. I'll never let another day go by that I don't tell her what she means to me.

Allison hops off the counter and reaches for the hem of my t-shirt. I lift my arms above my head, so she can rid me of it. She throws it on the bathroom floor on top of her dress. She runs her hands down my chest, working her way toward the button of my shorts. She peers up at me, biting her bottom lip. I nod, letting her know this is her show, and I'm just along for the ride. She unbuttons my shorts, making quick work of the zipper, soon they're sliding to my feet. I kick them to the side and crush my mouth to hers. As I'm kissing her, I stroke my hands up and down her back, not making any attempts to take anymore of her clothes off, although I want to, I won't push her for more.

Allison withdraws from our kiss and reaches behind her and unsnaps her bra. I watch her with hooded eyes as she removes one strap and then the other off her shoulders. I can't breathe, I can't move. She throws her bra onto the pile of clothing, then starts to remove her panties. I realize I'm standing here, like a fucking idiot, when I could be helping the sexiest girl I've ever seen out of her clothes. I place my hands over hers and kiss her neck; I travel my way past her breasts. Stopping to kiss the swell of each, I look up to gauge her reaction. Allison's biting her lip, watching my every move. Never taking my eyes from hers, I gently suck one of her nipples into my mouth nipping, sucking, and licking. She closes her eyes and moans. I move over to the other breast, wanting to make sure I give all areas of my girl equal amounts of attention. I continue on past her breast, kissing and licking my way down her toned abs. When I reach her panties, I slowly slide them down, placing gentle kisses on her hips, thighs, and legs. Her legs are shaking, and I have to help her step out of them. Good, she's just as affected as I am. I could hammer nails with my dick, I'm so hard for her again.

As soon as I have her panties off, she's pulling at my shoulders for me to stand up. I stand and capture her lips with mine, again. I could spend hours just kissing this girl. I'm so consumed with kissing her, it takes me a minute to realize her hands have made their way to my hips and she's attempting to rid me of my boxer briefs, which are currently tented beyond belief. I back away from her and finish pulling them down and kicking them off. "Allie, you are so fucking beautiful." I hug her tightly, because I can't seem to get her close enough. It's at this point, I admit to myself I'm gone, fallen. Little Miss Allison Shay Hagan owns me, and I'm okay with that. I never thought it would happen, but now that it has. Now that I'm hers, I couldn't be happier.

I push myself away from her lips, reach over, and start the

shower. Once the water is warm enough, I step under the spray and hold my hand out for her to join me. "Careful, baby, it's slick."

Allison takes my hand and steps inside. I clasp my hands on either side of her small waist and turn her back to the spray, so she can get her hair wet. I step back a little, and turn her back around to keep her under the spray of warm water while I reach for her shampoo. She looks over her shoulder at me with questioning eyes. "I promised I would be good, remember," I tell her as I begin lathering her hair, massaging her scalp.

She looks up at me and crooks her finger for me to come closer. I lean down. "What if I don't want you to be good?" she whispers. *Fuck me.* I want nothing more than to lift her up, wrap her legs around my hips, and claim her as mine, but I'm determined to earn her trust, and I want our first time to be special.

I kiss her neck, and then tilt her head back to rinse the shampoo from her hair. I reach for her loofa and lather it up with her body wash. I begin washing every inch of her skin. I can feel my dick getting harder by the second, and I didn't think that was possible. I have been with a lot of girls, but I've never showered with any of them. This is a new experience for me too, and it's one I hope we're able to repeat often. After rinsing her, my hands make their way back to her sweet spot. I gently stroke her, I want her to come. I gently insert one finger, then two. Fuck, she's tight. She braces her hands on my chest as I snake my other arm around her. "I got you, beautiful, just let go, I'm right here to catch you." That's all it takes. My lips collide with hers to stifle her moans. I hold her slick, wet body in my arms while she floats back to the here and now.

Allison reaches for my body wash and loofa. We don't speak, just watch each other closely. She begins running the loofa over my chest, arms, and back. She makes her way to my waist, but doesn't use the loofa as I'm expecting. I feel her small hands fist my erection. I feel like I could blow just from her touch. This amazing girl has once again rendered me speechless. I watch in fascination as she explores my length with her small hands. There is a slight tremble in her grip, but she doesn't let it stop her from exploring.

She looks up at me, biting her lip. "Will you help me? I'm not sure what to do, and I want to return the favor for you."

I caress her cheek. "I did that for me just as much as I did it for you. I wanted to feel your wet heat against my skin. To watch you fall apart in my arms."

"Please, Liam, I want this," she says as she continues to lightly stroke my cock.

I'll never be able to deny her anything. I gently place my hand around hers and begin moving it up and down my length.

CHAPTER TWENTY-ONE

Allison

LIAM PLACES his hand over mine and together we begin stroking his length. This is yet another first for me, and I have no idea what I'm doing. Yeah, I've read about it, but to be holding him in my hands is a little overwhelming. Not to mention, the desire that's pooling in my belly. Liam just brought me to orgasm for the second time within the last hour, and I want to do this for him. I want him to know I want him. To my surprise, I'm not embarrassed to ask him to show me. I feel so comfortable with Liam. We've spent the last two months getting to know each other. I know he would never push me to do something I'm not ready for, but I am ready for this. I want to make him come with my hand. After I get the rhythm down, Liam moves his hand to brace himself against the wall of the shower. I'm expecting him to keep guiding me, but he doesn't. He's letting me know this is my adventure, and he's just around for the ride. He starts moaning my name, just a whisper from his lips, "Allie," which fuels me even more. I lower myself to my knees and continue stroking him.

"I'm close, baby," Liam groans.

Then he erupts in my hand, his come coating my hand and chest. I continue to stroke him until he's done. He leans his entire body against the shower wall. I suddenly have the urge to taste him, something I've read about in my romance novels, but never thought was something I would do or have the desire to do. That is until I become engrossed in all that is Liam MacCoy. I lean forward and kiss the tip of his erection, licking him with my tongue. Before I can go any further, Liam's pulling me to stand with him, merging his lips to mine.

"Holy shit." He sucks in a deep breath. "You, beautiful girl, are now responsible for the two most erotic moments of my life." He holds me tight and kisses my temple. Liam washes himself again and leaves the shower for me to do the same.

I turn off the shower and pull back on the curtain. Liam's standing there wearing nothing but a towel around his waist, holding a towel open for me. He offers me his hand and helps me step out, then places the towel around my shoulders and begins helping me dry off. "You okay?" he asks me as he begins drying my hair with a second towel.

Am I okay? Is he kidding me right now? "More than okay." I stand on my tiptoes and kiss him until I'm breathless. "Thank you for another first, well, several firsts, actually." I am overwhelmed with emotion. The last several months seem like foreplay building up to the last twenty-four hours. It's still hard for me to wrap my head around all that has happened. Liam has shown me nothing but patience as I navigate this new world of intimacy that we share.

Liam smiles. "I like giving you your first. It's only fair since you're my first girlfriend. The first girl I've ever cared about that's not related to me." He turns me around to dry my back. "I've never showered with anyone before."

I'm not able to speak for fear of my voice cracking. Liam just admitted he has feelings for me. I know it's crazy and I've only known him a few months, but I'm falling in love with him. I knew it was a risk. I can only hope, when he decides this relationship isn't what he wants anymore, I'll be able to bounce back from my shattered heart. I try to shake the negative thoughts away. Liam has never given me reason to think he'll leave me, it's just hard to believe someone as wonderful as him would decide to change his ways for a girl like me. I'm going to embrace this relationship for as long as I have him and hope it never ends.

I follow Liam out of the bathroom and watch as he makes his way to his dresser and starts getting dressed. I follow suit and place my duffle on the bed, to pull out the clothes I packed for tomorrow. Liam walks up behind me and hugs me tight. "You need to bring more clothes to leave here, babe, that way you'll have options." I look over my shoulder at him and smile.

I drop my towel and start getting dressed in my shorts and tank. My cell phone, sitting on his dresser, rings. "Can you answer that?" I ask Liam.

He picks up my phone, swiping the screen. "Hello," he pauses, listening to whoever it is. It can only be a handful of people, but my guess is Hailey. "No, Hales, you called the right number. Allie's right here, hold on a sec." Liam walks back to the bed where I'm just finishing with my shorts. "It's Hales, baby," he says as he hands me my phone and drops a kiss on my temple.

"Hello."

"OMG, baby, did I just hear my brother, the womanizer, call you baby?" she asks loudly into the phone. Liam's still standing beside me and can hear every word. He laughs out loud and hollers back.

"You're damn right I did!"

"Did you hear that?" I ask her.

"Yes, holy fucking shit. He's whipped, and it's only been a day. Props to you, my friend."

"Hailey, that's just crazy," I try to reason with her.

I feel Liam's breath, hot on my other ear. "Actually, it's not. You own me, beautiful girl."

I'm speechless, I can hear Hales saying my name, but I can't respond. I'm staring at Liam, who's now standing in front of me. He gently takes the phone from my hand.

"Hey, Hales, no, she's fine, I think I just stunned her speechless," he says to her.

Liam shrugs, like Hailey can see him. "I just told her me being whipped isn't crazy." He smiles at me, an affectionate smile that resembles—love? No, that couldn't be, could it? "Then I told her she owns me," Liam tells her like it's yesterday's news. "Anyway, listen, Allie and I are just going to hang out here tonight. A few of the guys are coming over to play cards and watch movies. Why don't you come on over? You can try out the new futon I bought for you today."

I can only assume Hailey is again questioning his futon purchase. "I want Allison with me, always, and I need to make sure my little sister also has a comfortable place to sleep that does not include you shacking up with Aiden, we discussed this earlier, remember. Listen, Allie is spending the night, and she packed a bag, but needs more clothes. Can you bring her another outfit for tomorrow? Great, thanks, see you soon." He sets my phone back on his dresser.

I smile at him. "I guess we're staying in."

He places his hands on my hips. "I really just want to hang out with you, but we can do anything you want. Hales would have ended up here, anyway."

I wrap my arms around his waist and lay my head on his chest. "It actually sounds great." I peer up at him. "I just want to be with you."

Liam kisses the top of my head. "Let's go get you some food." We make our way to the kitchen, where we find Aiden standing with the refrigerator door hanging open.

He turns to face us and smiles. "Allison, how much do you love me?" he asks. I feel Liam tense beside me as he draws me tighter to his side.

"What do you want?" I ask him, snaking my arm around Liam's waist. I can tell by the tone of his voice he wants something.

"I'm hoping, maybe, you might, possibly, want to make us some of your famous enchiladas?" he asks sweetly, batting his eyelashes at me.

I shrug. "Sure, if you go to the store and get what we need."

"Yes. Liam, man, you don't know what heaven is until you've had her enchiladas, they're the bomb."

Liam looks down at me. "Actually, I think I do," he says only loud enough for me to hear.

Aiden leaves for the store, so Liam and I cuddle up on the couch to watch some TV. We end up watching Wedding Crashers on HBO. The last thing I remember is lying down on the couch with Liam bound tight in his arms.

I wake up to someone brushing a piece of hair behind my ear. I open my eyes to see Liam watching me. I'm curled up tight against his chest. "Hey, beautiful." I blush.

"Hey." I start to pull away, but Liam stops me.

"I'm not ready to let you go," he whispers as he runs his fingers down my cheek. I hear voices in the kitchen, voices I don't recognize.

"What time is it?" I ask him.

"It's a little after eight." This time I do jump up.

"Shit. I was supposed to make enchiladas. People are already here?" It comes out as a question, but I already know the answer from the voices and commotion in the kitchen.

"Yeah, Blitzen and a few of the guys got here about thirty minutes ago." He shrugs.

"Why didn't you wake me up?"

Liam pulls me off the couch, lacing his fingers with mine. "Because I was enjoying having you in my arms and wasn't ready to give that up."

I just shake my head. Liam has to be the sweetest guy on the planet. There's no way I can even fake being upset with him.

"Come on, boyfriend, you can watch me make dinner."

A huge grin spreads across his face as we make our way into the kitchen. We walk in to find Aiden, Hailey, Blitzen, and the two guys from The Warehouse last night, Mike and Scott. Wow, was that really just last night? So much has happened since then.

"Hey, sleepy-head," Hailey says to me.

"Hey." I can feel my blush coming on. Did they all see us sleeping? Of course, they did, you have to pass the living room to get to the kitchen.

"What's got you grinning like a mule with a mouthful of briars?" Blitzen asks Liam.

Liam draws me back into his chest and kisses right below my ear. "This beautiful girl just referred to me as her boyfriend for the first time." He holds nothing back.

"Boyfriend," Scott and Mike both say at the same time. Blitzen and Hailey don't know the specifics, but, by the look on their faces, they aren't surprised.

Liam nods. "Yes, boys, I'm officially off the market."

They both start talking at all at once. I'm not sure who says what, but comments range from "Fuck me", "holy shit", and "I'll be damned". Liam seems oblivious too, or just doesn't care about their shocked expressions.

"So," Aiden says, obviously trying to break the ice, "are you still planning on making enchiladas? I bought enough to triple the batch." He offers me a boyish grin.

"Yes, I'll make you your enchiladas." I sigh, like it's a huge inconvenience, but I have a smile on my face. I enjoy cooking.

"Well, I brought the stuff to make a triple layer chocolate fudge cake. So, you boys go do whatever it is you do while us women slave in the kitchen for you." Hailey ushers Aiden toward the living room.

All the guys, except for Liam, follow suit. "Um, that means you too, big brother," Hailey chides him.

Liam has yet to let me go. "You need any help, baby?" he asks me, completely ignoring Hailey's demands.

I shake my head. "I'm good, I've made this a million times. Besides, Hales has got my back."

Liam twists me in his arms and kisses me slow and sweet. "Let me know if you need anything." Then he turns and joins his friends in the living room.

CHAPTER TWENTY-TWO

Liam

I MAKE my way out to the living room still sporting a goofy ass grin on my face. I can't help it. Allison is mine, after weeks of agonizing, she's mine. I stop just outside the living room in the hallway. I know as soon as I enter the living room, the boys are going to give me shit. Honestly, I couldn't care less. I'm more concerned they'll say something about Allison that'll piss me off. I don't want to punch any of my friends, but I will. I take a minute to get my shit together.

I walk into the room. "There he is, Mr. Pussy Whipped himself," Blitzen says with a grin.

I walk behind the chair he's sitting in and slap the back of his head. "Watch your fucking mouth when you talk about me and my girl, fuckstick!" I hope getting it out there early will prevent further outbreaks of their diarrhea mouths.

Scott speaks up, "So, you really have a girlfriend?"

"Yes," I reply, not wanting to get into it with him.

"She seems like a cool chic. She's hot as hell," Mike adds.

I want to yell at him, but he's right. Allison is hot. Instead, I glare at him and change the subject. Much to my relief they roll with it. "So, what are we playing?"

"Texas Hold 'em," Aiden responds dryly. He always whines about losing too much money. He so needs to work on his poker face.

We'd just gotten through our first hand when Hales and Allison join us. There's only one extra chair without bringing in another from the kitchen, and I'm fine with that. Hailey sits in the chair next to Aiden as I tug Allison onto my lap and kiss her shoulder. She relaxes against my chest while I continue to play my hand. Having Allison here with me like this is a dream come true. I keep touching her, my fingers splayed out across her belly. My other hand is playing with her hair, or rubbing circles on her thighs; I can't control it. This makes playing cards difficult. I keep laying my cards down to touch her. I can see the looks my friends and sister are giving me, but frankly I don't give a flying fuck. I'm happier in this moment than I can ever remember. *Did I mention my girl is amazing?*

After about twenty minutes, Allison tries to get up, but I hold her still. She looks over her shoulder at me. "I have to take the enchiladas out of the oven," she says with a laugh.

I nod. "You need help, babe?" I ask her.

"No, Hales will help. We have to get the cake out too," she replies in a soft voice only I can hear. I turn her in my lap and kiss her slow and sweet, an act that's quickly becoming my favorite pasttime. When I pull away, her face is flushed. I kiss her on the temple and remove my arms from her waist, so she can get up. Hailey sees her get up and follows suit.

I turn my head and watch her walk out of the room. When I turn back around, I see my four friends doing the same. "Hey, you fuckers, that's my girl and my little sister, look away."

Aiden chuckles. "Sorry, man, no can do. Hales is hot, and since I just watched you paw at my sister for the past twenty minutes, I'm not going to turn my head when Hales gets up to walk out of the room."

I glare at him, but don't say anything. I know that he's right. I just don't want to admit it.

After dinner, which is delicious, we sit around playing our guitars and singing. We end the night watching movies. We start out watching The Hangover and end with Wrong Turn. Allison's curled up in a ball on my lap with her face buried in my shirt. *My night is perfect.* Halfway through Wrong Turn I realize she's fallen asleep. I gently lift her up off the couch and turn to Hales. "Night, Hales." I then look at Aiden and the rest of the guys and nod as I carry Allison to my bedroom.

I know I can trust the guys with Hales, besides Aiden will protect her, just like I would. I know they were checking her out, Hales is beautiful, but they would never touch her. They know Aiden and I would beat the shit out of them if they did. Aiden and I've been inseparable for the past four years, and he has grown close with Hales and my parents in that time. He sees Hales as a little sister, just like he does Allison; at least that's what he tells me.

Once in my room, I gently lay Allison on the bed before going to close and lock the door. I return to the bed to find Allison curled up in a ball. I retrieve my football jersey out of the closet and begin to slowly undress her. I have her shorts off, and I'm gently lifting her up to remove her top. I want her in my jersey. Caveman, I know, but I still see the images of her wearing Aiden's. I want to erase that memory from my mind. Allison is my girl. As I lift her up, her eyes open.

"Liam? What time is it?" she asks groggily.

"Shh, baby, it's late and you fell asleep. I'm just getting you changed for bed." She sits up and lifts her arms over her head. I gently lift her tank and pull it off. I go to place my jersey over her head, but stop when I hear her soft voice.

"This too." She's pulling at the strap of her bra. I nod because speech is not possible. I gently reach behind her and unhook her bra and slide it off her shoulders. Allison bites her lip, and I can tell she's nervous. Hell, I'm nervous, even after what she shared this afternoon.

She lifts her arms, and I slide her into my jersey. Again, I'm too over-come with emotion to speak, instead I tug the covers back and motion for her to slide in.

As soon as she slides under the covers, she curls back up on her side, facing away from me. I stand here for I don't know how long, just watching her. There's an ache deep in my chest. I don't know how it happened or when it happened, but this beautiful girl means the world to me. I'm brought out of my trance when a soft voice whis-pers, "Are you coming to bed?" Allison's looking at me over her shoulder with concern written on her face. God, I love this girl... Wait! *Holy fuck! Am I in love with her?* I love her smile, her voice, the way she takes care of everyone. I love that she's mine and I'm the one who'll be holding her tonight, and I'm the one she'll be waking up to tomorrow. *I'm in love with Allison.*

Instead of panic, I'm elated. I love her, and even though she may not be ready to hear it, I know it's true. What a difference embracing your feelings can make. Shit, if I'm being honest, I think I fell in love with her the day we met. There's no other explanation for the way I was consumed by her from the beginning. Never in my life have I felt this way. I start to wonder if Allison feels the same way. When she looks at me I can see affection, but is it love? I'm not sure, but I'm going to spend every day from here on out telling her how beautiful and amazing she is. Maybe in time she'll love me, as long as she remains mine, I can deal with anything.

I turn off the light, slide into bed, and tug the covers up over us. I reach for her as she moves back to rest against my chest. I drape my arms around her and kiss her on top of the head. "Goodnight, beau-tiful girl," I sigh with content. Finally, she's where she belongs. We lie here quietly, enjoying being in the moment for quite a while until I can feel her body relax and I know she has fallen back to sleep. "I'm never gonna let you go," I whisper before sleep claims me.

CHAPTER TWENTY-THREE

Allison

I WAKE up feeling like I'm being crushed. I open my eyes, and it all comes rushing back to me. Liam. I'm lying flat on my back, and he's sleeping soundly with his head on my chest, arms around my waist, and his leg thrown over mine. I can't prevent the smile I know I'm wearing. He held me in his arms all night. I glance out the window and it's still dark outside, good. This gives me some time to watch him in the shadows. I move my hand to his head and begin running my fingers through his hair. Liam has taken me by storm; body, mind, and heart. I was worried he would want more from me before I'm ready and even that he's 'playing me' to get into my pants, but he's treated me with nothing but love and respect. Love? I highly doubt it's love, but I can tell he truly cares for me. The way he looks at me, touches me, holds me. He makes me feel cherished.

I can feel myself falling harder and faster by the minute. I'm scared as hell, but I'm going to go with it. I'm going to paint my colors on the canvas of life and see how the picture turns out. My greatest hope is Liam and I can continue on this journey together.

I continue running my fingers through his hair, watching him sleep, when a loud clap of thunder rumbles through. Not expecting it, I jump, and Liam bolts up. "Allie, what's wrong?" I can't contain the laugh that escapes me.

"Nothing, the thunder just scared me, I wasn't expecting it," I tell him as he pulls me into his arms.

"Did it wake you up, baby?" he asks softly as he strokes his fingers across my back.

"No, I was awake," I reply just as softly.

"What? Why were you awake? Are you okay?" he asks.

I giggle at how concerned he is for me. "Liam, I'm fine. I was—I was watching you sleep." I reach up and run my hands through his hair. "I was doing this, and memorizing everything I can about you." I decide honesty is the best policy. Well, almost, I refuse to tell him I think I'm in love with him. Hell, to the no. That would scare him off for sure.

"I thought I was dreaming, but you're really here," he speaks softly, his breath tickling my neck.

"Yes, I'm here. You can go back to sleep. I'm sorry I woke you." I curl tight against his chest.

Liam tugs the covers back over us and kisses the top of my head. "Can we spend the day together?" he groggily asks me. I'm not completely sure he's not talking in his sleep. I hold in the chuckle that wants to escape me. I don't want to wake him again if he's sleeping.

"I want nothing more," I reply honestly.

I lie here against his chest, feeling the rise and fall for several minutes, before I start to feel my eyes grow heavy. I shift a little, settling in further, and feel Liam's grip tighten on me. Safe in his arms I drift off to sleep.

I wake up to the sound of pouring rain and pounding thunder. I reach across the bed for Liam, but he isn't there. I hear a soft chuckle and the sound of the door closing. I look over to find Liam walking toward me, carrying a tray full of food.

He sets the tray on the side of the bed. "Good morning, my beautiful girlfriend." He leans down to kiss me. "Did you miss me?" he asks cockily.

"Always." I decide he needs to know the truth. I'm so far gone when it comes to him, and he needs to know he has the power to tear me apart. "Why were you laughing?" I question him, although I have a pretty good idea.

He smiles at me. "I saw you reach for me. The pout on your face once you realized I wasn't in bed was adorable." He taps the tip of my nose with his index finger. He then proceeds to feed me bites of fresh fruit and French toast.

"This is amazing, did you make this?" I question between bites.

"Yes, beautiful, I did. I wanted to do something special for you." He laughs. "Hales, however, is not too happy she had to take over and finish for her, Blitzen, and Aiden. I was in a hurry to get back to you."

I lean in to kiss him on the lips. "Thank you for making me breakfast in bed."

"I have to admit I kind of had an ulterior motive." He winks at me.

"Oh, yeah, and what might that be?" I ask as he feeds me my last bite of French toast.

Liam sets the tray on his nightstand. "Well, I have an amazing, beautiful, sexy girlfriend, and I'm hoping I can convince her to spend the rainy day in bed with me."

I bite my lip, am I ready for that? "Liam—"

He places his fingers over my lips. "Baby, I just want to hold you and spend time with you. When we make love for the first time, we'll be alone, and you'll be one hundred percent certain you are ready to take that step. All I need is you, beautiful girl." Then he kisses me soft and slow. We kiss for what seems like hours, only stopping long enough to catch our breath before our lips merge once again.

Liam's so gentle and caring with me. Touching me everywhere, caressing me, but never taking things too far. Honestly, I want him to take things further. I crave the way he makes me feel. I'm also really enjoying making out with my boyfriend. This isn't something I've experienced, so it's nice to lounge around in his bed kissing, touching, and getting to know each other more intimately. We also talk a lot. Liam tells me about the draft and how nervous he is. I don't want to think about that. As of this morning, I'm able to admit to myself I'm in love with him. When he gets drafted and has to leave me, I'm not sure how I'm going to cope. I knew going into this I would get my heart broken, but it didn't stop me from forging ahead. I guess we'll cross the bridge when we come to it. Liam tenses up when we talk about him moving away. I can tell it's not something he's looking forward to, now that we're together. We still have several months before we need to worry about the draft. I'm going to take it one day at a time.

I'm currently wrapped in Liam's arms, his front to my back. We've decided to take a nap when there's a light knock at the door. "Go away," Liam growls at the intruder.

I can't help it, I giggle. In retaliation, Liam starts to tickle me, and my giggle turns into full blown laughter. "Uh, guys, ready or not, here we come," Hailey says as she swings the door open. Liam releases me, and I try to gain my composure.

Hailey shakes her head. "Hey, love birds. Aiden and I are headed to Mom and Dad's for lunch, are you two coming with us?"

"No," Liam growls at her. "We're staying in this room all day. Tell Mom and Dad we said hello." With that he draws me tight into his arms and kisses my shoulder.

Aiden appears behind Hailey. "He said no, didn't he?" he asks her.

"Yep, the beast has been tamed." They both roar with laughter.

"You're damn right I have, now get the hell out, so I can take a nap with my girl." He then throws a pillow at the door.

Hailey and Aiden back out and shut the door. I can hear them laughing all the way down the hall. "Liam, we can go to your parents' if you want."

"I don't want. I want to lie here with you in my arms. I want to enjoy the fact that you're mine, and I no longer have to lie here in this exact spot and wonder what it would feel like to hold you. I can do it, and that's all I want. Allison, you have no idea the effect you have on me. I'm consumed by you, and until forty-eight hours ago, having you here was a dream. You've now made my dream a reality, and I'm not ready to step outside this bubble of happiness. The football season is gearing up, and my time with you will be cut short with away games, school, and practice." He leans over me, so he can look in my eyes. "I just want to be with you today, baby."

I nod in agreement because words fail me. If there were ever any doubts that I love him, his last little speech washed them all away. Liam holds my heart, and I'm scared as hell to tell him.

CHAPTER TWENTY-FOUR

Liam

TIME IS FLYING BY. Allison and I have spent every spare minute together. We've adjusted to our life as a couple rather seamlessly. We've received several questioning stares around campus, but I couldn't care less, they'll get used to us and move on to someone else soon enough. Tonight is the first football game of the season, and I'm stoked to have my girl in the stands. Last night she stayed over, since she doesn't have class on Fridays. We've spent the entire morning together. It was the perfect way to spend the day before my first game of my final season of college football.

I just finished zipping up my equipment bag when Allison comes walking out of my bathroom. She smiles at me, which makes my heart kick into overdrive, just like always. She begins to get dressed and starts looking around, like she's lost something. Which she has, I hid the shirt she'd picked out to wear, because I want her to wear my jersey. I want everyone there to know she's mine.

"Babe, have you seen my shirt?" I smile at her calling me babe. We've settled quite well into our relationship.

"Yep, I hung it back up in the closet." I smile sweetly at her.

"Why would you do that?" she questions as she heads toward the closet. I reach out and grab her hand.

I take a deep breath, why I was nervous I have no idea. "I was actually hoping you would wear this." I hold up my away jersey.

She smiles at me, her emerald eyes sparkling. "You want me to wear your jersey?" She drapes her arms around my neck and kisses me deeply. "Can I tell you a secret?" She waits for me to respond. I nod. "I really wanted to wear it, but I wanted you to ask me. I didn't want to be *that girl*. You know the one who parades around wearing her boyfriend's jersey, staking her claim."

I tuck a loose hair behind her ear. "Baby, you are not *that girl,* you're *my* girl, and you staking your claim would make me very happy." Then I kiss her, trying to convey to her that she means everything to me. The past few months have been the best of my life, even before she was mine. I can't picture my life, my future, without her in it. I still have yet to tell her I'm in love with her. Several times it's almost slipped, but I want the moment to be right. I want her to always remember it. I'm hoping all goes well for our trip to my parents' beach house tomorrow, and I can tell her then. I need her to know what she means to me.

Allison has slept in my jersey several times, and that, too, is a vision I'll always remember. Today she's just as beautiful wearing it with her jeans and tennis shoes. She has her hair pulled into a side ponytail, my name and number clearly visible on her back. She also has a small number seventeen on her cheek. I kiss my number. "You're beautiful," I tell her as I lead her out of our room and down the hall. Aiden and Hailey are ready and waiting.

When we arrive at the stadium, we have to part ways, so they can get to their seats while Aiden and I hit the locker room. Their seats are prime real estate, right behind the team on the fifty yard line; I want her as close as I can get her. I kiss her soundly before leaving her. It'll be several hours before I can taste those lips again. Cat calls and whistles come from my teammates walking by. I raise my hand to wave at them before kissing Allie on the forehead and leaving her there with her face flushed with embarrassment, and Hales laughing her ass off. She's going to have to get used to being in the spotlight. I'm talked about to be a first-round draft pick for the NFL, and she's a permanent part of my life as far as I'm concerned. She'll have to ignore the attention.

The season opener is kick-ass. We beat Ohio State University thirty-four to twenty-two, and I couldn't be happier. I send Allison a text telling her and Hailey to meet Aiden and me at the main entrance. Her reply is, 'hurry your fine ass up, I need a hug.' I laugh, of course, I'm going to hurry. There's nothing I want more than to wrap my girl up in my arms.

As we approach the entrance my eyes immediately start scanning for the girls. When I spot them, I'm overtaken by anger. The high I was feeling from our win instantly dissolves. Hales and Allie are leaning against the wall, and those fuckers, Jason and Todd, are standing in front of them, blocking them in. I can see they're trying to be cordial, but are uncomfortable with the situation. I look over at Aiden; he's obviously just as pissed off as I am.

I step behind Jason, place my hand on his shoulder, close to his neck, and squeeze as hard as I can. His knees buckle as he turns to face me. He throws his arm back, like he's going to punch me, and I catch it mid-air. Aiden's standing toe-to-toe with Todd, neither of them moving.

"I suggest you leave my girl and my sister alone, unless you're yearning to get your ass handed to you again," I snarl at him.

"Fuck you! You're all talk. Hit me and see where you land with the NFL," he spits back.

I grip his arm tighter in my hand. I can see the tension in his jaw; I'm hurting him. Good, after what he did to Allie, he's damn lucky I haven't unleashed my wrath on him. "You listen to me, and listen good, mother fucker. Those girls are my life, so don't you think for a second the NFL, or anything else, is going to keep me from protecting them."

I look over and see Hales and Allie are both tucked in close on either side of Aiden, he has his arm around each of their shoulders. Todd has his hand on Jason's shoulder, trying to pull him away from me. I stretch my arm that isn't touching him out toward Allie. I immediately feel her small hand grip mine, only then do I release my hold on Jason. I pull Allie as close as I can get her, Aiden does the same with Hales. "The next time I see you anywhere near either one of them, I'll beat you within an inch of your life," I seethe.

Jason stares at me, not moving and not saying a word. Todd's still trying to pull him away silently. A campus police officer walks up. "Hey, MacCoy, Emerson, everything all right here?" he asks in an authoritative voice.

"We're all good, these guys were just leaving," I say back to him, never breaking eye contact with Jason. They both nod at the security guard, turn, and walk away.

I draw Allie close and hug her, like my life depends on it. I pull away and tuck a loose strand of hair behind her ear. "You okay, baby?"

She nods yes as she turns to look at Hales. I refuse to let go of her, so I move closer to where Hailey and Aiden are standing. I keep one arm around Allie and the other reaches for Hailey; she doesn't make any attempt to come to me. Aiden has her clutched tight to his side. I rest my hand on her shoulder "You alright?" She simply nods.

I nod at Aiden, a silent communication of me letting him know I appreciate that he has my back protecting Hales. I hug Allie again and kiss her on top of the head. "Let's stay in tonight, instead of going out, we can order pizza." She looks to Hailey for her approval, who nods in agreement, and with that we are headed home. I call and order delivery on the way there, so the pizza will arrive about the same time we do.

Back at the apartment, Aiden and I grab quick showers. I walk out of my room the same time Aiden walks out of his, and I follow him down the hall toward the living room. I suddenly bump into him, and when I look up he has his finger to his lips to tell me to be quiet. I raise my eyebrow in question as he mouths 'listen' to me.

We stand still in the hallway and listen to the girls. I feel bad for eavesdropping, but I know this might be my chance to find out what really happened with those two fuckwads. Don't get me wrong, Allie would tell me if I asked her, but I know she'll play it off as no big deal, trying to diffuse my anger.

"Allison, I'm so sorry for all of this. If I never would've dated Todd and talked you into doubling with us and Jason, none of this would have ever happened," Hailey tells her.

"Hales, this isn't your fault. They're pompous assholes, who like to hear themselves talk. Jason can tell me all day long that he's a better man than Liam, he's just spouting hot air because I know better," Allison replies.

"No, really. I knew Liam didn't like them, and I also knew he was into you. I should have seen this coming," Hailey argues.

"Regardless, when Liam found out about Todd, he would've had the same reaction. You're his sister, and he loves you," Allison tries to reason with her.

Hailey sniffs. "I thought Todd was a nice guy, I should have listened to Liam. AGHH! Why can't I just have the guy I want? I see what you and Liam have, and I want that. I want what you have."

"What I have is a mess. I'm madly in love with Liam and I'm just waiting for him to realize being in a relationship isn't what he wants."

Hailey squeals, "You love him? When did this happen, you've so been holding out on me."

"Shh!" Allison tries to get her to lower her voice. "A while now, I'm so afraid to tell him. I'm afraid it'll push him away. God, Hales, he has the power to crush me."

"Allison, you're so blind. Liam loves you, crazy girl. Trust me, he's just as scared as you are."

I hear Allie sniffle, and I can't take it anymore, I need to wrap her in my arms. I go to move around Aiden and he stops me. Holding up his finger for me to wait.

"So, you still crushing on—" Allison tries to speak, but Hailey interrupts her.

"Stop, don't say it," Hailey warns her. "Yes, I want him, but it can never happen, so let's just leave it at that."

"But—" Allison is again interrupted.

"Allison, leave it alone," Hailey warns her.

I'm not waiting any longer. We've heard way too much as it is, and I need to hug my girl. How can she possibly not know I'm madly in love with her? I tell her every day how amazing she is. I'm ready to forget about my plans for tomorrow and tell her right now, but I still want it to be special. Allison deserves special, she's my heart.

I take off down the hall, ahead of Aiden, who's chuckling behind me. He knows it's killing me not to be near her. *Bastard*. I walk into the living room and head straight for Allison. She looks up at me and smiles, and I feel my heart squeeze at the sight of her. She's sitting on the love seat. I lift her up and pull her into my tight embrace. She wraps her arms around my neck. God, this girl is my life, I'll never be able to get enough. I bring her lips to mine and kiss her slow and sweet, savoring her.

I hear Aiden behind us. "Take it to the bedroom, Mac. I don't need to see you sucking face with my sister." He laughs. The doorbell rings, so he goes to pay for the pizza.

I sit down on the love seat with Allison curled up in my lap. We stay this way the rest of the night, only moving long enough to fill our plates or to grab something else to drink. I need her as close to me as possible.

After a couple of hours of laughing, and talking about the game, I notice Allison keeps yawning. I'm beat, myself, from the game. I'd like to say that is my motivation for calling it a night, but really, I just want to be alone with my girl.

CHAPTER TWENTY-FIVE

Allison

WHEN LIAM ASKS me if I'm ready for bed, I'm quick to agree. This has been a long ass day, and I'm ready to curl up with him and kiss it goodbye. He picks me up, we both say goodnight to Hales and Aiden, and then he carries me to his room. I smile at the thought, Liam refers to it as our room and gets offended anytime I call it his.

"What are you smiling at, beautiful girl?" he whispers in my ear.

"Just thinking about how much I love being with you." *Oh, shit.* I said love. It's true I love him, everything about him and our relationship, but I don't want to scare him off. Maybe he didn't notice.

Liam gently sets me on his bed and drops to his knees in front of me. He gently holds my face in his hands. "Baby, every single second I spend with you is precious to me." He pauses, like he wants to say more, but doesn't, instead he kisses me.

I open my mouth, inviting him in. I'll take any and every part of him he offers until he no longer gives me the option. Our makeout sessions are becoming hotter and hotter, and I want him. I want to feel him inside me. I've told Liam this on several occasions, and he keeps putting me off, telling me he wants me to be sure. I argue it's my virtue and I can do as I please. Currently, I'm begging Liam to take me, and still he turns me down. "Please, Liam, I want you," I whisper into his lips.

"Baby, I don't want you to have regrets. Your virginity isn't something you can ever take back," he says as he continues his assault on my body with his lips.

I tug at the hem of his shirt, wanting it off of him. I need to feel his skin against mine. He raises his arms, allowing me to pull off his t-shirt. I lift my arms over my head, letting him know what I want. He slowly pulls my shirt off and rids me of my bra. I wrap my arms around his neck and pull him as close as I can. I bury my head in his neck and melt into him. There's nothing in this world that compares to being skin on skin with Liam, wrapped tight in one of his hugs.

"We really should sleep. I want to get started early tomorrow," he whispers.

I whine my protest, but move away from him, so we can get ready for bed. I know he's right, but I want him. Tomorrow night there's no way in hell I'm letting him turn me down. Hailey went with me the week after we started dating to get on birth control. I haven't even told Liam yet. He always shuts me down. Well, not tomorrow. I want him to be my first. I finish undressing with the help of Liam, and he slips his t-shirt he had on over my head. We brush our teeth and crawl into bed.

I snuggle into his side as he brings the covers up over us. I feel Liam kiss the top of my head. "Goodnight, beautiful." I fall asleep in his arms, feeling safe, loved, and happier than I can ever remember.

The next morning, I wake up to Liam kissing my belly. My hands instantly find his hair and I begin to run my fingers through it. Liam lifts his head and smiles at me. "Good morning, beautiful," he says in his husky not quite awake voice. He kisses his way back up until his lips find mine. He kisses me slow and sweet in the way only Liam can. He moves to my neck and whispers in my ear, "I need to taste you." I can't help the moan that escapes me at his words. Liam smirks at me as he finds his way back down my body. Instead of removing my panties, he simply moves them to the side as his tongue touches me in the most intimate of ways. This is not new to us. Liam has performed this, shall we say 'act', several times since we became official. I still struggle with the intimacy of his face and his mouth being *there*. Liam reassured me after the first time I'm the most beautiful girl he has ever seen and he'll never be able to get his fill of my taste. Yeah, so when those sweet words are whispered intimately, what do I do? I melted, that's what I did. I caved and haven't said a word about it since.

I can feel my release building as I lift my hips. Liam knows I'm close and increases his efforts by inserting one finger, then a second. That's all it takes for me to explode with my passion for him. Liam rides the wave with me, then kisses his way back up to my neck. I push him on his back and start kissing his bare chest. He tries to pull my mouth to his, but I have other plans. I know he won't make love to me, no matter how much I beg him. Not here anyway, with Aiden and Hales just down the hall. I, however, want to give him release, just as he did for me.

I make my way down his rock-hard abs, kissing and licking until I reach the 'V' of his hips. Courtesy of hours in the gym and being on the football field. He's so damn sexy, and I want him, all of him. I carefully slide his boxes down over his erection, which stands proud. At least I know he wants me too. I'm still a little unsure of my abilities of what I am about to do, I've only done it a couple of times. I gently kiss the tip of his erection before licking the full length of him. He moans his appreciation.

"Allie, baby, you don't have to do this," he pants. This is what he says to me every single time. Liam's always more concerned about me.

Of course, I ignore him and take as much of him as I can in my mouth. I start out slow and easy, gradually increasing my speed. Liam places his hand on the back of my head, but he never forces me. He simply rests it there, as if he needs another connection between us. I never imagined I would enjoy this, but with Liam, I not only enjoy it, I ache for it. I love him with everything I am, and to be this intimate with him, to bring him to release with my mouth, is indescribable.

"I'm close, baby," Liam murmurs.

I moan and take him as deep as I can, knowing the vibrations in my throat will send him over the edge. I feel his release warm and salty in my throat, and I swallow. I don't release him from my mouth until I feel him relax against the bed. He hauls me up to him and kisses me hard.

"You. Are. The. Most. Amazing. Girlfriend. Ever," he proclaims between kisses.

I pull away from him and smile. "You're not so bad yourself, MacCoy," I say with a wink.

Liam's in a hurry to get to the beach house, so we shower quickly and are on the road before six a.m. We leave Hales and Aiden a note, explaining we want to get a head start and we will see them late tomorrow night. The drive to Wilmington only takes a little over three hours. We stop along the way to eat breakfast at Cracker Barrel. We don't talk a lot during the drive, but the silence is pleasant. I think we're both just trying to grasp that we're about to be alone, completely alone, for more than just an hour or two. For me, I'm thinking of how I'm going to seduce him. I want to know what it feels like for him to be a part of me. He owns me heart and soul, and I want to be connected to him physically in every way possible.

We make it to the beach house just after ten in the morning. The house is breathtaking. There's really nothing outlandish that stands out, except for the view. I stand at the double glass doors and stare out at the ocean. I feel Liam as he drapes his arms around me, his front to my back. He kisses my temple.

"This view is spectacular," I tell him.

I feel him nod. "It really is. This place belonged to my grandparents. They gave it to my parents for their tenth wedding anniversary. We've spent so much time here it really is our second home."

I lean back against his chest, just enjoying being here with him. He's all mine for the next twenty-four hours, and I'm ecstatic. "So, the water is too cold to really swim, what did you have planned for us?" I ask him.

Liam turns me, so I'm facing him, still locked tight in his arms. "Honestly, I just want to spend time with you, no interruptions. Anything else you decide you want to do is just a bonus," he says as he leans in for a kiss.

I smile against his lips. "I don't want to leave this house until we have to."

Liam smiles in return. "Well, then, I'm glad we stopped at the store on our way in." He hugs me tight. I love Liam's hugs.

We agree to unpack our supplies, and then prepare lunch. We decide on spaghetti and meatballs, that way there'll be plenty of left-overs for dinner tonight as well. Liam turns on the radio, and we begin cooking together. We don't talk a lot, we don't need to. Just being with one another, sharing the simple task of preparing a meal, we're both smiling from ear to ear. Liam continues to find little ways to touch me. His hand on my back while he reaches above me in the cabinet. A kiss on the temple while offering vegetables from the salad he's making. He even swats me on the ass when I'm bent over, looking in the refrigerator. I can't help but think about how it would be if we lived together. Sharing duties, making dinner, beginning and ending our days together indefinitely. In my mind, I can see the life we'd build together, and I want that, I want him. I just wish I had the nerve to tell him, my fears of pushing him away prevent me from pouring my heart out to him.

We eat lunch on the deck, enjoying the view of the ocean. Liam suggests we take a walk on the beach. As soon as we have our mess in the kitchen cleaned up and the leftovers packed away, Liam grabs me by the hand and leads me down to the water's edge. The sun's starting to set by the time we start our journey back to the beach house. We walk hand in hand, talking about anything and everything for hours. Liam expresses his fear of the NFL, and I open up to him about my fear of being truly and utterly alone in the world.

Liam stops and pulls me close to him, gently cupping my face in his strong hands. "Allie, you aren't alone. There are so many people in this world who love you." He pauses, gauging my reaction. "I love you," he whispers right before he merges his lips with mine in the most passionate kiss of my life. I can feel his emotions in every touch of his lips, every swipe of his tongue. *Holy Shit! He loves me!* I throw my arms around his neck and deepen our kiss. I need to taste his lips. This amazing man loves me and has told me for the first time when he knows I need to hear it the most. The moment is perfect, and I want to embed every single detail to my memory. I never want to forget this feeling.

Liam slowly ends our kiss as he rests his forehead to mine. We're both breathing heavy. After taking a minute to catch my breath, I place one hand over his heart while the other gently caresses his cheek. "I love you too, Liam. So much." I'm looking into his beautiful blue eyes and watch as they soften at my words.

A huge smile breaks out on his face as he picks me up and spins me in circles. We're both smiling and laughing when he finally places me back on my feet. I shiver from the cold night air that's setting in. Liam rubs his hands up and down my arms. "Let's get you back to the house, beautiful girl."

Back at the house, I heat up the leftovers while Liam builds us a fire. We settle on the floor at the coffee table to eat our dinner. I watch Liam eat and, hell, even that's sexy. I know I want to be with him, and now that I know he loves me, the want has increased tenfold. Liam has one hand on my thigh while he eats with the other, and the sensations of him rubbing circles there is driving me insane. He doesn't know it yet, but he's only increasing my need to seduce him.

After dinner we sit by the fire. I'm sitting in between Liam's legs, my back to his front. We're enjoying a glass of wine and just being in the moment. Liam hugs me tight in his arms. "I meant what I said,

Allison." I turn my head to look at him. He runs his finger down the side of my face. "I love you with everything in me. I never thought I could feel this way. You make life better, you make me better. I can't imagine my life without you in it now." He kisses my temple.

Oh, my. I can't form words. There's a huge lump in my throat, and I'm fighting back tears, tears of joy. I wish there was a way I could show him how much he means to me. How much happiness he brings to my life. I was lost before Liam, and now I know exactly where I am. Anywhere he is, my heart and soul are there as well. I get up on my knees, still between his legs, and brace my hands on his cheeks. "Liam, you are my heart. I've been so afraid to tell you, because I thought it would push you away." I lean in close to his lips, never breaking eye contact. "I love you." Then I kiss him. I try to show him how much he means to me through touch, with the caress of our tongues.

Liam pulls away and smiles softly. "Why don't you head up to shower and call Gran while I clean up, then we can curl up in bed and watch a movie?" I nod in agreement, kiss him quickly, and head off toward the shower.

CHAPTER TWENTY-SIX

Liam

I WATCH Allison skip off to the shower and take a deep breath. *She loves me.* I was waiting for the right moment this weekend to tell her how much I love her, but when she started talking about being afraid of always being alone, I couldn't hold it in. As long as I breathe, she'll never be alone. This girl means everything to me, and I'll spend each day of forever showing her just how much.

I make quick work of loading the dishwasher and cleaning up the kitchen. I race off to the bedroom to find my girl sitting on the bed with a towel around her body and one twisted around her head with the phone to her ear. She's smiling as she listens to whatever it is her gran's telling her. I have yet to meet her gran, but I can tell she's an awesome lady. I kiss her on the cheek and tell her to tell Gran hello as I head for the shower, giving them time to finish their conversation.

I hurry through my shower, only taking the time to slide into a pair of boxer briefs when I'm done, not wanting to waste one minute of time being away from her. She's still talking to Gran. I don't want to interrupt her; I know how much Allison misses her. I slide in behind her on the bed and remove the towel from her head. I grab the brush that's lying beside her and gently begin brushing her hair. I see her shoulders relax at my touch.

She finishes her call with the promise to Gran that we'll both be there next weekend for a visit. I tell Allison to pick out a DVD as I slip my t-shirt over her head, and then make my way to the kitchen to make us some popcorn.

I hop up on the bed and pat the spot next to me for her to climb in. "So what movie did you pick?"

Allison smiles sweetly up at me. "The Notebook."

I groan in protest, but in all honesty, we could watch the fucking Weather Channel for all I care. As long as she's in my arms, I'm a happy man. Six months ago, if you would've told me I would be madly in love and passing up going out with the guys just to be around her, I would've said you were an idiot. Things change, and I've learned to expect the unexpected in all things love and Allison.

I can feel her laughing beside me at my mock annoyance. I put my arm around her and bring her close. *God, I love this girl.*

I think we're about halfway through the movie, honestly, I can't be sure. I've spent the entire time watching Allison. She truly is the most beautiful girl I've ever seen, and she loves me. I've been touching and kissing her since the movie started. I can tell I'm distracting her, but, honestly, I don't care. Just being in her presence is distracting to me. I try to be good and keep my hands to myself, so she can watch the movie, but then I remind myself she's seen it before. *In that case, game on.*

I snuggle closer and place soft kisses on her neck. She tilts her head to the side to give me better access. I smile. I continue kissing and licking while running my hands up and down her thighs. She turns around, pushes me on my back, and straddles my hips. I reach for the remote and turn the TV off. I don't want to hear anything but her. I sit up with her in my lap, and she binds her legs around my waist. I take her face in my hands. "I love you, beautiful girl." I kiss her slowly at first, nipping at her bottom lip, running my tongue across it. Then I slowly push my tongue between her lips, exploring her mouth, savoring her taste. I pull back and wait for her to open her eyes and look at me. "Allison, you mean everything to me. I can't imagine life without you. I miss you when I'm not with you—all I do is think about you..." I pause to get my emotions in check. I was on the verge of losing my shit, and I need to get this off my chest first. She needs to know what she means to me. "Look in my eyes and you will find me, look in my heart and you will find you, my heart beats your name. You have taken up permanent residence inside me, eternally. I'm never going to let you go."

Allison's gazing into my eyes, with soft tears running down her cheeks. I kiss them away before finding her lips with mine. I flip us over on the bed, so I'm lying on top of her, my weight balanced on my forearms.

Allison runs her hands through my hair. "I don't want you to ever let me go. I wish..." She pauses, collecting her thoughts as I stroke the tears from her cheeks. "I wish I could find the words to express to you how much you mean to me." She brings my lips to hers and kisses me like her last breath depends on it. "Let me show you," she whispers against my lips as her hands trail down my back, stopping at my boxer briefs. She begins tugging to pull them off. I sit up and discard them, and when I turn back to the bed, her arms are in the air. I lift my shirt over her head and throw it across the room.

I climb back on the bed and position myself on top of her. I can feel her heat against my erection. I need to calm the fuck down, before I push her into something she's not ready for. I try to pull away, but Allison grabs my arms.

"Make love to me, Liam. I want to feel you inside me. I want to know what it's like to be one with you. I love you," she breathes against my lips.

I stare into her emerald eyes, and I can see love and passion. I don't see any signs of hesitation; she wants this with me. This amazing girl is giving me something she'll never be able to give another. I swallow hard over the lump in my throat. I'm losing my shit again, and this time, I don't want to hide it. I want her to see how her gift is affecting me, how she affects me.

Allison smiles up at me. "Liam, you are my soul, I belong to you. I want to share this with you, and only you."

"You're mine," I whisper against her lips. I slowly move my way down to her breast, taking my time with each one. I move my hand to her center and can feel she's ready for me. It's then it hits me. "Shit," I say against her neck.

"What?" she croaks out.

"I don't have a condom. I didn't bring you here for this. I just wanted to be with you, alone," I tell her.

Allison embraces my cheek and lifts up, so I'm looking at her. "Liam, I'm on the pill," she tells me.

I look at her in question so she continues on. "The week after we became official, Hailey went with me to the clinic. We're protected."

"Babe, I would've gone with you," I tell her. I want to be there for her in every way.

She blushes. "I wasn't sure we would make it this far, but I wanted to be prepared if we did."

I rest my forehead against hers. "I'm clean, I just had my annual before the semester started, and I haven't been with anyone since months before then."

"I trust you, Liam." I can tell there's a deeper meaning behind those words.

I nod my head and position myself between her legs. I stop to take in the moment. I'm overwhelmed with want, passion, and need for her. I'm also a little intimidated.

"What's wrong?" she asks me, concern and what looks like insecurity lacing her face.

"It's just that, well, I have never done this before, not without a condom. This is a first for me, for a couple different reasons," I tell her honestly. She nods her head, so I continue. "I've also never made love before. It was always just sex, release, but you—you're different.

My heart and soul are engraved with you. I'm scared as hell to hurt you and scared if we do this and you regret it I'll lose you and, well, that's just not an option for me."

Allison raises her hips to meet mine. "I want you with everything in me, I want you in me." She smiles softly. "You've branded my heart. There's nothing that can keep me away from you. You're a part of me. I want this with you, to share this part of me with you. I love you." She lifts up and kisses me soft and slow. "Please, make love to me."

My resolve crumbles, and I nod, letting her know I'm in this with her. "Baby, this is going to hurt, and I'm so sorry. Once I'm all the way in, I'll stop, so you can adjust to me. If you need me to stop or you change your mind, tell me, okay?"

"I won't want you to stop, but yes, I promise."

With those words, I gently begin pushing my way into her slick folds and have to grit my teeth as soon as I feel her heat. The feel of her with no barrier between us emotionally or physically is a feeling I'm not prepared for. I'm glad I saved this moment, this feeling for her. I watch her closely, gauging her reaction as I continue to slowly slip inside. Allison raises her hips to meet mine. "More, Liam, please," she begs me.

"Easy, babe, I don't want to hurt you."

She's shaking her head. I'm so focused on watching her face, caught in the moment, I don't realize she has wrapped her legs tight around me, until she thrusts against me, pushing me the rest of the way inside.

She gasps in pain, and I hold completely still. "Are you okay?" She doesn't answer, so I start to pull out.

"Please," she whispers. "Please, don't, I want you. Please, make love to me. I'm fine, it just hurt for a minute."

I lean down and kiss her, hoping to relay the emotions coursing through me. This moment has changed me. Allison is mine and I'm hers, I'll never feel this with anyone else. I begin to move slowly at first, increasing my efforts as she begins to moan my name. I can feel my release rapidly approaching, so I balance my weight on one hand while my other finds her center and begins to stroke her folds while I increase my rhythm.

"Liam."

"Allie."

We both shout at the same time. I gently rest my full weight on her, not that there's currently another option. I'm not ready to be disconnected from her, and my orgasm has taken everything out of me. As I lie here breathing, like I just ran a marathon, I lift my head slightly to look at my girl. She's smiling, satisfied and sated. "I love you," I whisper against her lips.

"Oh, Liam." She hugs me tight against her with her arms around my neck. "That was the most amazing moment of my life. I can't explain it." She hugs me tighter.

I rise up and gently remove myself from her. I hop off the bed and go to the bathroom. I come back with a wet cloth. "Open for me, baby," I say as I caress her leg. I gently wipe away her arousal and mine, then throw the cloth back through the bathroom door. I climb up on the bed and take her in my arms. "This," I say, motioning with my free hand between us, "is the most exhilarating experience of my life. Everything with you is brighter, happier, more fulfilling." I kiss her temple. "I love you so much," I say, squeezing her tight.

"I love you too," she says with a yawn.

I kiss the top of her head and reach over and turn off the bedside lamp. I reach down and pull the covers up over us. I fall asleep with the love of my life in my arms, and I can't remember ever feeling more content.

CHAPTER TWENTY-SEVEN

Allison

THE MORNING SUN is just starting to peek through the blinds. I'm lying on Liam's chest with his arms holding me tight against him. I gently tilt my head, careful not to wake him up. I watch him sleeping. He's so handsome. My mind drifts to last night and the things we shared. I never in a million years ever dreamed I could be this happy. Hailey and Aiden are still in awe of how much he's changed, but to me he has always been my Liam. Always protecting me and telling me how special and beautiful he thinks I am.

"Why are you staring at me, beautiful?" Liam asks in his oh so sexy morning voice.

"Just taking in the view," I cheerily reply.

"What's got you so happy this morning?" he asks as he tickles my side.

I laugh out loud while squirming away. "I'm just really happy," I gasp between laughs.

Liam tightens his hold on me. "You aren't going anywhere," he says as he flips over on top of me, resting his weight on his arms by my head. He's looking at me with a huge grin on his face, the one he reserves for me.

"What's got you so happy this morning?" I throw his words right back at him, still laughing from his onslaught of tickling.

"That's the most beautiful sound, I love hearing you laugh." He gives me a chaste kiss. "As for my happiness, let's see; I made love for the first time to the most beautifully sexy woman I've ever met, I held her in my arms all night, and I wake up to her still in my arms and the sound of her delightful laughter. That, my beautiful girl, is the short list of why I'm so happy this morning." He then kisses me with so much passion I'm ready to go another round. I lift my hips to his, letting him know what I want. Liam pulls away from our kiss breathing heavily. "Baby, it's too soon. I know you're sore, and I don't want to hurt you."

"I'm fine, I can deal with it. I want you," I beg him.

Liam shakes his head. "We can't, baby, I don't want to hurt you." He kisses my forehead. "Let's get in the shower and grab some breakfast before we head home."

I grumble my agreement and let him pull me off the bed. He's right I am sore, but the pleasure of being with him is so worth any amount of pain.

The next several weeks are a whirlwind of happiness. I introduced Liam to Gran as my boyfriend. To say that she's happy for us is an understatement. Sometimes I feel like I need to pinch myself to make sure that I'm not dreaming. Our relationship has evolved and I love him more every day. As soon as we both stopped fighting it, everything just fell into place. Liam and I spend as much time together as possible. I spend more time at his condo than the dorm rooms. Hailey is there as well. The four of us just kind of fit together as one big unit.

School is out for Thanksgiving break, so Liam and I spend a lot of time together. Thursday, Liam, Aiden, and I are having Thanksgiving dinner with Gran and Aiden's parents. I also invited Hailey to join us, since their parents are waiting until the next day to do their Thanksgiving dinner. So, here we are on Wednesday night driving to Gran's. Liam's going to stay at Aiden's while Hailey stays with me and Gran. Gran didn't say this needed to be the arrangement, but out of respect for her, we've decided this is the best way, even though we hate to sleep without each other.

As soon as Liam pulls into Gran's driveway, I'm out the door and running to see Gran. It's been three long weeks since I've seen her, and I miss her so much. I hear Aiden laughing behind me as they unload our bags for the night. I barrel through the door. "Gran, we're here!" I yell for her.

"I'm in the den, Allie girl," she calls back.

I reach the den and drop to my knees in front of her chair and engulf her in a hug, careful not to hurt her. Gran is the constant in my life, and I miss her. I pull away and kiss her on the cheek just as Aiden, Liam, and Hailey enter the room. Aiden walks over to Gran and hugs her. I hold my hand out to Liam while motioning for Hailey to come over as well.

Liam and Hailey say hello to Gran. They both give her a gentle hug and I can feel my chest expand with love for all three of my best friends.

"Thank you all for spending the holiday with me. I'm so glad my Allie girl has met such nice friends," Gran says as she turns to face Aiden. "And you, it's been way too long. I think I'm going to need another hug," she tells him with a smile.

Aiden quickly obliges her as the rest of us take a seat. We sit and talk to Gran for a few hours until it's obvious she's completely worn out.

"Guys, I'll be right back. I'm just going to help Gran get settled," I tell them. I help Gran ease out of her chair and lead her down the hall to get ready for bed.

"You love him," she says matter of fact.

"Yeah, I really do. He and Aiden have been best friends since

Aiden's first year of college. He's such a great guy, Gran." I blush from my onslaught of gushing over Liam.

"He loves you too, you know," she states. "He's the color on your canvas."

I feel tears prick my eyes at her referral to what she has told me since I was a little girl. *Life is a giant canvas, Allie, and you should throw as much paint on it as you can.* I nod my head to agree with her. "Yeah, I really think he does, and I think he is. He tells me every day how beautiful he thinks I am and how much I mean to him," I tell her as I finish helping her into bed and kissing her cheek goodnight.

"Follow your heart, sweet girl. It will lead you to happiness."

"Goodnight, Gran. I love you." I kiss her cheek again.

"Goodnight, Allie girl."

When I get back to the den everyone is exhausted from the long day, it's after midnight. Hailey and I walk the guys out to the porch.

"So, dinner will be ready at one, so don't be late," I tell them.

Aiden laughs. "Mom will be here early to help cook. Do you really think we're going to pass up a big home cooked meal?" he asks me, like it's the craziest thing he has ever heard.

"Can I do anything to help you?" Liam asks me.

"Holy shit, you're more whipped than I thought," Aiden says, punching Liam in the arm and laughing.

Liam smiles. "You're damn right I am, my girl comes first, always," he says, kissing me softly. He pulls away and rests his forehead on mine. "Sweet dreams, beautiful girl." Then he kisses me again, slow and sweet. I could stand here all night, but Aiden and Hailey clearing their throats brings me back to reality.

"Goodnight," I whisper against his lips with one last chaste kiss.

Hailey and I head to bed as well. I have a queen bed in my old room, and she's going to be sleeping with me. *I wish it was her brother.* Once we're settled, lights off, and everything is calm, the realization of how used to sleeping with Liam I really am sets in. He must have been reading my thoughts because my phone vibrates on the nightstand with a new message.

. . .

LIAM: I miss you. I can't sleep without you.

ME: I miss you too.

"IS THAT MY BROTHER?" Hailey questions me.

I'm glad it is dark, so she can't see me blush. "Yeah," I reply.

We're quiet for several minutes, my phone buzzes again.

LIAM: I love you, baby. Sweet Dreams.

ME: I love you too.

"HE REALLY DOES, YOU KNOW."

"He really does what?" I'm confused as to what she's referring to.

"Liam, he really loves you. I heard him talking to our parents, he told them that you're 'the one'," she says.

I swallow the lump in my throat. "The one?" I question her.

Hailey laughs softly. "He's different with you, better."

I debate on what I should tell her. She's his sister, but she's also my friend. I decide to go with honesty without the intimate details of our relationship. "I love him so much. I really feel like he's my soul mate. Is that crazy? We've only been together a short amount of time."

"No, it's not crazy. I wish I could say I had found 'the one'."

I don't respond as my mind drifts to Liam and the depth of my feelings for him. In such a short amount of time he has become my world. I have to admit I'm a little worried about the draft and how those events will affect us. I try not to think about it and just enjoy the time I have with him.

"There's this guy that I have kind of had a thing for, for a while now," Hailey speaks into the darkness of the quiet room. "He doesn't see me the same way, but I would give anything for him to look at me the way my brother looks at you." She reaches over and grabs my hand. "I'm so glad he has you and that you and I have become friends. Both of our lives have been changed because of you."

"I love you both," I whisper through the cloud of tears in my eyes. Neither one of us says anymore as we drift off to sleep.

CHAPTER TWENTY-EIGHT

Liam

Let's just say last night sucked. It took me what seemed like hours to fall asleep and here I am wide awake at six in the damn morning. I'm so used to sleeping with my girl by my side that it's not possible for me to get a full night's sleep without her. I remember her telling me she had to be up early to put in the turkey, so I decide to text her.

Me: *Good morning, beautiful.*

I hold my phone tight against my chest anxiously waiting for her reply which comes rather quickly considering the time.

Allison: *Good morning. Missed you last night.*

Me: *I missed you too, baby. Did I wake you?*

Allison: *No, I am up had to put the turkey in can't get back to sleep.*

Me: *Can I come over?*

Allison: *Please.*

I hop out of bed, pull on a t-shirt and sweats, and head out. I open the door and run into a sleepy Aiden.

He looks at me confused. "Where are you going?" he asks, still half asleep.

I show him my phone, which has a picture of Allison on the screen. "Allie's up, she's putting the turkey on and can't get back to sleep, so I'm going over to keep her company." That's my story anyway. I know if I tell him I can't stand to be away from her a minute longer he would razz me about it all day. Although by the look in his eye, he already knows the real reason.

"What time is it?" he asks, rubbing the sleep out of his eyes.

"It's a little after six." I step to the left to walk around him and hear him chuckle behind me.

"Whipped bastard," he mutters as he laughs.

"Love sick bastard," I call back to him. Might as well call a zebra a zebra and not a horse, I'm madly in love with the girl and want to be with her every second of the day.

Allison's waiting at the door for me when I get there. I immediately pick her up and hold her close. She buries her face in my neck. "I missed you," I whisper in her ear.

She leans away, and I set her back on her feet. "Come in, I made coffee and cinnamon rolls."

We end up in the den, her on my lap, eating cinnamon rolls and drinking coffee. At a little after seven, Allie hears Gran starting to stir, so she goes to help her out of bed and into the den. While she does that, I make Gran a plate of fresh fruit and oatmeal and pour her a cup of black coffee. I have everything ready and waiting on the TV tray beside her chair by the time they make their way into the den.

"Liam—How did? How did you know?" Allison asks me.

I shrug my shoulders. "I pay attention and I listen when you talk."

She carefully helps Gran into her chair, then turns and launches herself at me. I catch her in my arms and hug her tight. "I love your hugs," she whispers to me. She pulls back and touches her hand to my face. "I love you more every day, you're amazing." Then she kisses me.

She kisses me full on lips with tongue right in front of her gran. I'm not sure how her gran feels about intimate displays of affection, and I don't want to disrespect her, but there's no way I can tell Allison no. We'll just have to ask for forgiveness later. Allison pulls away and smiles at me. I'm lost in her eyes, the emotion I see in them. She finally breaks the trance when she pulls me to the couch and plops down beside me, never letting go of my hand.

"Allie girl, can you get me my medication?" Gran asks her. Allison nods, gets up, and walks toward the kitchen.

I'm a little nervous, I just made out with this woman's granddaughter right in front of her and now she's obviously trying to get me alone. I clear my throat and rub my hands together. My palms are sweaty.

"Liam," her gran says my name so softly I almost don't hear her.

"Yes, ma'am?" Okay, now I'm really worried.

"You love her, you love my Allie?" she questions me.

I nod my head vigorously. "I do, more than I ever thought possible," I tell her.

"Good, can you promise me something?" she asks. Her voice is laced with so much emotion, sadness or concern, maybe. I can't really tell.

"That depends, ma'am. If you're going to ask me to stay away from Allison, I'm sorry I just can't do that." I'm not sure what she's going to ask of me, but I'm sure it has to do with Allison and me. Agreeing to stay away from her isn't an option.

Gran laughs softly. "No, I see the way you look at her and her at you. I would never take that away from either of you." She smiles at me. "Although, after your statement my fear of what I'm about to ask you is no longer palpable." She reaches her hand out to me, so I stand up and walk over to her chair. I kneel down in front of her, taking her hand in mine while her other rests on my cheek. "Take care of her for me, Liam. I'm her only family and, well, I won't be on this earth forever. All Allie has ever wanted was to have a family." She pauses and takes a deep breath. "I was never able to give that to her. After her parents died, it was just us. It has always been just us. I need to know she'll have someone who will be there for her forever after I'm gone." She's looking at me as if she can see inside my soul. "Can you love her for me, give her the life she deserves?"

I have to fight to hide the fact that her words have me choked up. Allison's grandmother is asking me to love Allie forever, to give her the family and life she has always dreamed of. I have to gather my wits before I can respond. "I love Allison with everything I am. She has changed my life in ways I never thought possible. I want nothing more than to spend the rest of my life with her. I'm honored I have your blessing." I lean over and kiss her cheek.

Gran nods, tears in her eyes. "I met my late husband and knew by the end of our first date he was the one. Love like that is hard to find. I see it in the two of you."

I hear Allison and Hailey coming down the hall. I nod my head, letting her know I'll cherish Allison always and rush back to the couch. When Allison walks in, she offers me her genuine *I'm happy* smile. The one she reserves for me, I smile back. The old Liam would have been out the door and running for the hills after that speech. The new Liam is elated to have her blessing. I want to go look at rings today, although I know that's not possible. Allison and I have talked about the draft, but never what it's going to mean for our relationship. To me, it doesn't change things, I love her. I've spent a lot of time thinking about this, and I want her to go with me. I need her with me always. I've been afraid to broach the subject with her. Afraid I would be pushing things too far too fast, but after last weekend, my mind is made up. Allison is mine, always, and I'll do everything in my power to show her she belongs with me. I can give her the love and the family she has always wanted. My mind veers to a pregnant Allison, and I have to readjust my position to hide the evidence of my erection. I want it all with Allison. I want to give her the family she's always craved.

The rest of the day goes off without a hitch. Hailey, Allison, and Aiden's mom make dinner while Aiden and I keep Gran entertained. Aiden's mom made the desserts. She really outdid herself, but Aiden and I graciously volunteer to take the extras back with us. Hailey and

I clean up the kitchen while Allie and Aiden spend time with his folks and her gran. We stay in the kitchen longer than necessary, giving them all time to visit.

———

"SO, how you feeling about the draft?" Aiden asks me later.

I shrug. "I'm nervous, man. How about you? Nervous?"

He nods. "Yeah, I am. I mean, coach says you and I are in line for first round picks. It would be bad ass if we could go to the same team."

I laugh. "Hell, yeah, it would, but the chances of that happening are slim and none."

Aiden clears his throat. "So, what about you and Allison?"

"What about us? I love her, man. You know this," I reply defensively.

"That's obvious, dude. You're different with her. What I meant is how do you think the two of you will do with the long-distance thing?" he questions.

I'm shaking my head no before he even finishes his sentence. "I don't want to do it. I can't be away from her for that long." I hesitate before telling him more, but he is my best friend, who just happens to have been her best friend first. If anyone can tell me how they think she'll take my suggestion, it would be Aiden. "I want her to come with me." I hold my hand up to him to keep him from talking. "I know it would be a lot to ask, but fuck, man, she's like the air I breathe. I would support her and help her finish school, or not, she can just travel with me. She can do whatever she wants, just as long as I get to come home to her every night and wake up with her every morning."

Aiden raises his eyebrow at me. "Wow," is all he says. Maybe it's all he can say. In the four years we've been friends, I've never talked about a girl and forever.

"Do you think she'll come with me?" I ask him so softly I'm surprised he heard me.

"She loves you, but it'll be hard for her to be that far away from her gran," he tells me.

"I know, man, I thought about that. I want Gran to come with us. I want Allison with me always, and Gran is her family, I want them both to come with me." This is something I'd decided earlier today when Gran gave me her blessing to love Allison with everything in me. She deserves the same, and I would give those two the world if I could.

Aiden nods his head. "Then, yeah, I think she'll go with you." He curses under his breath. "We better get drafted to the same damn team. I'm losing both my best friends." He hesitates then he says, "Uh —what about Hales?"

"What about her? I assume she'll stay at UNC and finish out her degree."

Our conversation is cut short when Allison and Hailey come walking into the kitchen. I can tell something is off by the look in her eyes. She walks toward me, and I open my arms wide for her, welcoming her into my embrace. "What's wrong, baby?" I ask her.

"It's time for us to go, but I hate leaving her," she speaks so low I can barely hear her.

I hug her tighter. It takes all the willpower I can muster not to tell her when I'm drafted she and Gran can come with me and be together all the time. I know now isn't the time, but seeing her sad is tearing me up inside.

CHAPTER TWENTY-NINE

Allison

SAYING goodbye and leaving Gran always causes an ache deep in my chest. She insisted I go to college and experience life. I never really wanted to go to college. My parents' life insurance left me enough money that I never have to work. Don't get me wrong, I don't want to be some spoiled princess blowing through money, never having a job or responsibilities. I have dreams for my future, just not the same as other nineteen-year-old girls. I want a family of my own. My dream is to be a wife and a mother surrounded with family and love. All the things I lost at the young age of ten. Gran did the best she could, but growing up with your ill, elderly grandmother as your only family, well, it's lonely.

When we arrive back at Liam and Aiden's apartment, Hailey immediately crashes on her futon, Aiden crashes on the couch, and Liam and I stumble to his room. We go through our routine of brushing our teeth and changing for bed. I, of course, am in one of Liam's old t-shirts. We crawl into bed, and Liam immediately pulls me to him. I rest my head on his chest while he holds me tight with one hand and gently strokes my arm with the other. He sighs deeply.

"What's wrong?" I ask him, never moving from my spot on his chest.

"Nothing, baby, nothing at all. I just missed you last night. I barely slept, and now you're here in my arms, in our bed where you belong. I'm just happy," he replies softly.

I sit up on my elbow to look at him. "Thank you for today, Liam. Spending the day with Gran, the house full of people, it's what I always wanted growing up. Aiden and his parents would stop in after their family things, but really, it was only ever Gran and me." I take my hand that's resting on his chest and bring it to his face, tracing his jawline with my fingers. "You made one of my dreams come true today. For the first time in as long as I can remember, I felt like I had a family." I scoot my body up, so my face is mere inches from his. "I love you, Liam MacCoy, so much." Then I kiss him. He immediately responds and moans as I slip my tongue past his lips. He rolls onto his side and pulls me close until we're wrapped up in each other's arms, legs entwined, lips fused, tongues battling as my heart bursts with happiness and love.

We pull back from the kiss, mainly due to the fact we both need to catch our breath. Liam gently brushes my hair behind my ear, stroking his hands across my cheek. "Allison, I need you to know I'll always do everything in my power to make all of your dreams come true. You and your happiness are the most important things to me." He pauses, staring deep into my eyes, neither one of us saying anything. It's almost as if he's searching for my acceptance of what he just told me. He must have found what he was looking for because he continues, "Baby, I want you in my life forever. I'm not proposing at this exact moment, but I'm going to. I need you to know what this is for me."

I feel tears leaking from my eyes, but I don't move to wipe them away. I'm afraid if I move, this moment will end, or maybe it isn't real, and I don't want to wake up if I'm dreaming. Liam wants me, forever.

He gently wipes the tears from my cheeks with his thumbs. His eyes find mine again and they're also glassy with emotion.

"Allison, I don't know what my future holds with the NFL. I know it's rumored I will be picked in the draft, how do you feel about that? Are you okay with being the wife of an NFL player? Because, baby, if you don't want that, I'll withdraw and start searching for jobs in sports medicine."

"Liam, the NFL is your dream. It's what you've always wanted," I counter.

He shakes his head no. "No, baby, the NFL *was* my dream. Now my dreams consist of you, you and me and a long happy life together wherever that may be. I refuse to make a decision about our future without you giving me your blessing. What do you see for our future, beautiful girl?"

I study him, this man who has completely captured my heart and soul. He's telling me he wants to marry me. That he'll give up his life-long dream just to make me happy, to be with me. Liam, the guy with a major fear of commitment, is telling me he's committed to me for a lifetime. I feel more tears roll down my cheeks. "I've never told you this, partly because I didn't want to scare you away. It's also not all that ambitious for a nineteen-year-old." He scoffs at that, but I keep going. "I've never had the desire to go to college. I'm here because Gran wants me to experience life and not taking care of her all the time. I've focused so much on school to honor my parents that I'm burnt out. My dream has always been to be a wife and a mother. I want a family, a house full of love and happiness. My parents, when they died, both had large life insurance policies. I received ten million dollars at the time of their deaths between the policies and the court settlement. I live off the interest." I watch his expression; he's simply listening to me, hanging on every word. "I could never allow you to give up your dreams for me, Liam."

"Allie, I can get drafted to a team hundreds of miles from here." He pulls me tighter against him. "I can't go into the draft knowing I'm going to be leaving the love of my life behind. I need to know that wherever I end up you'll be with me, by my side. I know it's a lot to ask, but none of it would mean anything without you there." He kisses my forehead. "We can bring Gran with us, she can live with us, and you guys can be together every day. Hell, we can build a house and give her her own damn wing; I don't care as long as you're next to me."

My heart is racing, beating so loud I'm sure he can hear it. I take his hand and place it on my chest, right above my heart. I can tell, by the expression on his face, he can feel my heart's thunderous rhythm. He places my hand on his chest in the same position, and I can feel his heart mirroring the beat of mine. I take a deep breath and repeat the words he said to me in the emergency room a couple months ago. "Liam, I'll go anywhere with you. You're my dream," I whisper. I watch as a single tear leaks from his eyes. I gently kiss it away. When I pull back, he's grinning so widely I think his face might crack.

"You're really mine, you'll come with me?" He swallows hard. "You'll marry me?" he asks softly.

I nod. I can't speak over the lump in my throat.

"I'll give you the perfect proposal, but just knowing you want a future with me, forever with me, you've made me the happiest man alive. I love you, Allison," he says as he draws me tight against him, and we fall asleep in each other's arms.

I'm jolted awake at seven by Liam's alarm clock screeching with its annoying beeps. I reach over and turn it off, then roll over to wake Liam up. "Liam, it's time to get up, babe."

He grumbles, "I'm awake," as he moves me back against his chest. "Good morning, beautiful," he whispers huskily in my ear. I snuggle back into his arms, seeking his warmth. "Do you remember last night?" he questions me. "Do you have any regrets in the light of day?"

I roll over so that I'm facing him. "No regrets, you're stuck with me, MacCoy."

"Allie, I promise to make all of your dreams come true," he says as he kisses me. I thought about protesting, since I haven't brushed my teeth, yet, but I know he doesn't care. Every morning I've tried to warn him, he acts as though I'm crazy. Going as far as to tell me he'll take me anyway he can get me. "As much as I wish we could lie here all day, I need to get up and get moving because we have to be at the field at nine. The game starts at noon, are you and Hales still coming with my parents?" he asks me.

"Yes, they're picking us up here, and we're all headed to their house for dinner afterward. Your mom made a huge meal just to wrap it up and put it in the fridge." I smile, thinking about Mrs. MacCoy going through so much trouble, so Liam and I could spend Thanksgiving with Gran. "I really appreciate her delaying dinner, so we could go to Gran's yesterday," I tell him.

"Baby, she loves you, just like I do. This works out great, so we can all be there to celebrate today's win." He winks.

I giggle at his cockiness. "That's the most beautiful sound," he says, kissing me quickly and rolling out of bed.

I slip on a pair of his sweats and head to the kitchen to make breakfast before they have to leave.

I'm standing at the stove, flipping pancakes, when I feel Liam step behind me and place his hands on my hips. "Can I help, baby?"

I look over my shoulder at him. "No, you just relax. You have a big game today."

He rests his head on my shoulder and guides my hips back against his. I continue making pancakes while he holds me close.

"Mornin'," Aiden mumbles as he slides into a chair at the table. "Ash, I just want to say you being with Liam, which leads to you being here all the time, which leads to you feeding us, has to be the best chain of events ever."

Liam and I laugh as I serve them their breakfast and place the extra batter in the fridge for when Hailey wakes up. "You look rough, man," Liam says as he slides into his chair next to me.

"I slept on the couch," Aiden replies with his mouth full.

"Why?" Liam asks him, perplexed that he would sleep on the couch when he has a perfectly comfortable bed just down the hall.

Aiden shrugs his shoulders. I have a feeling it has something to do with Hailey. He's very protective of her and he's always watching her. I think Hailey has a thing for him as well. Every time I try to talk to her about Aiden, she changes the subject. I make a mental note to keep an eye out for more clues from these two. Liam and Aiden scarf down their food. They have to be at the field at nine. I hear Hailey moving around in the living room, so I get up to start on her pancakes.

Liam removes the batter from my hands and sets it on the counter. He then picks me up and sets me on the counter beside it. He steps in between my legs and cups my face in the palm of his hands. "Thank you for breakfast." He kisses me. "I bought you a new hoodie to wear to the games, since it's getting colder. It's hanging in our closet." He winks at me. He's always referring to it as our room, our closet. I guess after last night and the decisions we made about our future, I should stop arguing the fact and embrace it. He kisses me again and it's a good thing I'm sitting, he literally makes me weak in the knees. He rests his forehead against mine. "I love you, beautiful girl. I'll see you at the game."

Hailey walks into the kitchen, Aiden behind her. "Damn, make sure you clean the counter," she scoffs. At that we all laugh. Liam kisses me one more time before setting me back on my feet, so he and Aiden can leave for the stadium.

———

WHEN WE ARRIVE at the stadium, we find the seats the guys have reserved for us and their parents, front and center, right on the fifty-yard line. Of course, this also has us sitting right behind the team. Liam says he likes knowing I'm so close. I'm a little nervous for the game, we're playing Duke, which means Liam and Aiden are playing against Todd and Jason. Neither Hailey nor I have heard anything from either one of them. I hope there's no drama today in the game.

We win the coin toss. I feel the nerves in the pit of my stomach as I watch Liam and Aiden line up on the field. Both Todd and Jason are defensive lineman, so guess what that means. Yep, they take the field as well. Liam currently has the team in a huddle; I can only imagine what he's saying to them about Todd and Jason.

At the snap, Liam shuffles his feet, throws his arm back, and launches the ball to Aiden. He catches it with ease, just before being smashed to the ground by two members of the opposing team. The hit is hard, and I stand waiting for him to get up. I feel a tight grip on my hand. Out of the corner of my eye, I can see Hailey gnawing on her lip with worry all over her face. Aiden slowly gets to his feet and the crowd roars, as he throws his hand in the air waving. Aiden then points to our group and smiles. I relax, and Hailey releases the breath she was holding. There's something definitely going on there.

The next two downs, Liam repeats the same play. He throws to Aiden who catches it, again with ease before being mauled to the ground. They're now on the twenty-yard line, and Aiden's getting the shit beat out of him. The line is doing a great job of protecting Liam, but I'm fearful for Aiden, he's taken three hard ass hits. They break from the huddle and take the line. I watch, holding my breath, to see if we can get the first touchdown of the game. I watch as Liam swiftly hands the ball off to Aiden, who then starts to run. It's at this point I realize they're pulling a quarterback sneak and Liam still has the ball. I go psycho fan girl and begin to scream, "Run, Liam, you got this, baby!" That's when others around me realize Liam still has the ball. The other coach yelling at his team to get the quarterback, but it's too late. Liam glides into the end zone, touchdown! I grab Hailey. We're jumping up and down and screaming. I belt out, "That's my man!" Yeah, not exactly my finest moment, but hey, my man just scored a touchdown.

Hailey and I are still hugging and talking about how awesome the play was when I feel a tap on my shoulder. I look over to see Mrs. Mac smiling widely as she points toward the field. Liam is running toward the sideline ball tucked under one arm, helmet in the other. I watch him as he nears, but doesn't stop, instead he by-passes his teammates and heads straight for me. I watch as he hands his helmet off to a photographer and scales the wall. He climbs over the side and grabs me with his free hand behind my neck and kisses me, hard. The kiss is brief, but doesn't lack once ounce of the passion we share. Liam rests his forehead against mine. "I missed you, beautiful girl." He pulls me in for a hug and kisses my temple. "See you in about an hour, baby," he says as he jumps back over the wall, takes his helmet back from the photographer, and waltzes back to the bench, like nothing happened.

Mrs. Mac leans in and bumps her shoulder into mine. "You make him happy, Allison. It thrills me to see him this way."

I smile at her, tears in my eyes. "I love him." I realize what I said and slap my hand over my mouth. Don't get me wrong, I'm not embarrassed of Liam or the love that we share, but holy shit I just blurted it out to his mom. I can feel my face heat with embarrassment.

Mrs. Mac just laughs. "He loves you too, Allison." She smiles and turns her attention back to the game.

CHAPTER THIRTY

Liam

I TAKE some ribbing from the guys on the team for my display with Allison. What they don't realize is she's my world. They can rib me all they want, but at the end of the day my girl is coming home with me, and they're going home alone.

We end up winning the game thirty-six to twenty-two. Not only am I coming off a win, but that fuckstick Jason broke his arm and will be out of the rest of the season. Serves the fucker right for what he did to Allison. *Karma is a bitch.*

Dinner at my parents' is great, as always, only this year I have a little something extra to be thankful for. I watch Allison as she helps my mom in the kitchen and talks to my dad about football. I can't take my eyes off of her. She's currently helping Mom and Hales wrap up the leftovers. Dad, Aiden, and I are in the living room talking about the game; only I'm not paying attention to the conversation, not when I can watch Allie.

"Liam," my dad says with a smile as Aiden smacks me on the

back of the head.

"Ow! What?" I bark at them. They're both laughing at me.

"Aiden was telling me that the guy who landed Allison in the emergency room broke his arm tonight in the game," Dad inquires.

I smile and say, "Karma," as I turn to look at Allison again. The memories of that night rushing back. The night I stopped fighting what I feel for her and made her mine. *Best day of my damn life.*

I feel a strong hand on my shoulder, and I look over and see it's my dad with a grin on his face. He nods his head toward the girls and Mom in the kitchen. "I remember when your mom and I first got together, I couldn't take my eyes off of her either."

I chuckle. "Dad, you still don't take your eyes off of her."

He's grinning while watching my mom. "She's still the most beautiful woman I've ever seen."

I nod. "I feel the same way about Allison, Dad. I love her with everything in me."

"I know you do, son, she loves you too. She blurted it out to your mom at the game today."

I try to control my grin, but it so isn't happening, not when it comes to Allison. "Any words of wisdom?" I finally ask him.

"Never let a day go by that you don't tell her what she means to you. Don't let money or fame or anything else come between you and the ones you love."

I nod, letting him know I understand. Nothing would ever be more important to me than her.

"I'm proud of you, son, you got a great girl there. Cherish her."

"Always."

Instead of driving back to the apartment, we stay at my parents'. Aiden's staying in the guest room, like he always does, and Allison is trying to tell me she's going to sleep in Hailey's room with her. *Yeah, not happening.*

She's concerned about disrespecting my parents. I hate to do it, but I finally have to bring Mom into the conversation.

"Mom, please tell Allison she can sleep with me." I realize how it sounds as soon as I say it. Allison's face goes red with embarrassment instantly. Aiden, Hailey, and my dad all bust up laughing.

Mom maintains her composure and smiles widely at us. "Allison, you and Liam are both adults and you love each other. We know this isn't something the two of you take lightly. We're fine with you sharing a room," Mom says it much better than I do.

Allison nods, not wanting to discuss the matter any further. We all say goodnight and head off to bed. Once we are in my room, I lock the door to ensure we have privacy. I tug Allison into my arms to kiss her, but she turns her head. "I'm sorry I embarrassed you, but there's no way I was going to have you sleeping with Hales and me sleep alone just across the hall."

Allison has yet to look at me, she's staring at the floor. I gently lift her chin. "I love you so much it kills me to be away from you. You're the best beginning and end of my day, every damn day." She's looking at me, but not saying anything, so I continue. "Falling asleep with you in my arms each night and waking up with you next to me each day…" I shake my head. "You're everything to me, my world revolves around you, and there's no way I could've gotten any sleep without you in my arms, especially knowing you were across the damn hall with Hailey." I rest my forehead against hers. "I'm sorry I embarrassed you, but I'm not sorry I fought for you. I'll always fight for you, for us." This time when I kiss her she kisses me back.

I lift her in my arms and gently set her on my bed. Without saying a word I lift her arms above her head and gently remove her sweatshirt. The sight of her takes my breath away as always. "Damn," I murmur. I can't believe she's mine. She stands up and lifts my shirt over my head, and then she makes quick work of her jeans. I follow suit, not wanting to miss a moment of what is yet to come. Allison scoots back on the bed and pats the spot beside her. I climb in, lying beside her, my hands instantly travel to her hips, so I can bring her closer. She rests her hand against my cheek.

"Liam…" She's trying to fight the emotion I can see filling her eyes. I wrap my arms around her and wait patiently for her to collect her thoughts. "You've changed my life so much. Thank you for all that you've given me. For loving me." A single tear drips from her beautiful eyes. I kiss it away. "I love you so much," she murmurs.

I kiss her soft and slow, gently stroking her tongue with mine. Her confession has me choked up, so words aren't really an option. If the guys thought I was whipped earlier, they should see me now. My man card would be revoked, no questions asked. I kiss her neck, her shoulders, making my way toward her breast, giving both equal attention. I shift, so I'm on top of her and her legs instantly fall open, inviting me in. I lace my fingers with hers and place our arms above her head as I gently enter her. *Home.* I continue to slowly slide in and out, making love to her. I watch Allison closely as she lies beneath me, eyes closed mouth open. I watch as she arches her back, and I can feel her tighten around me, I know she's close. "Open your eyes, beautiful girl." I wait for her to meet my gaze. "I want to watch you fall apart, I want you to see me lose myself inside of you." I continue my slow deep thrusts until I know we're right on the brink. "Come for me, beautiful." She tugs on my hand and places it over her mouth, it's then she falls apart, and I'm right there with her. I can feel her tighten around me, I can see her love for me in her eyes, and that's my undoing. I release myself into her. *Mine.*

I gently remove myself from her and roll onto my side, placing her back tight against my chest. I kiss her shoulder. "I love you, Allison Shay Hagan. I can't wait to spend forever with you." Then I fall asleep holding my future.

The next few weeks leading up to Christmas are crazy busy. Aiden and I have three away games in a row, which means time away from Allison. This makes me cranky as fuck, and my teammates and best friend make a point to tell me frequently. Allison takes the opportunity to spend more time with her gran, she would drive up, spend the night, and they would watch the game on TV. I can tell she's enjoying her time with Gran, so knowing she's safe and happy eases my temper a little.

Allison and Hailey work it out, so we'll spend Christmas Eve with Gran and Aiden's parents, and then Christmas Day with Mom and Dad. Aiden's parents are going on a cruise and leave Christmas Day. I don't care either way as long as I get some Allison time. I'm missing my girl.

We arrived at Grans on the twenty-first, and I'm dreading not being able to sleep next to Allison. I'm not sure how Gran will feel about it, so I've been building myself up to accept the fact that I'm going to have to fall asleep without her. I'm not looking forward to this. Hales came with us, so I'm sure she'll be sharing a room with Allison.

Aiden needs to finish his shopping, so he and I venture out to the mall, leaving the girls behind to hang with Gran. They plan on baking, just the thought of that makes my stomach growl. I'm done with my shopping. Hales and I went in together and got Mom and Dad a weekend away at a bed and breakfast. Aiden got a gift card to have his car detailed inside and out, *trust me, it needs it*. Hales got a gift card to the mall, the way she loves to shop I know this will make her happy. Allison and I bought Aiden's parents a gift card for a local steak house. For Gran, well, I convinced Allison we should get her a new flat screen TV. She doesn't leave the house, so I figure this would be a good gift. Hailey agreed. As for Allison, well, let's just say I did my best to spoil her. I bought her a Coach purse I heard her and Hales talking about. Hales, of course, helped me get the right one. I bought her a diamond heart necklace, because, well, the girl is my heart. I bought her new boots, a couple of outfits, and a day at the spa. Aiden also got this for Hales, so they can go together.

We end up in a jewelry store, so Aiden can pick up his mom's gift from his dad. He'd ordered it a few weeks ago and just got the call today that it was in. His dad found out we were coming here and asked us to pick it up for him. I'm browsing around while we wait and end up at the case filled with engagement rings. I'd looked at them when I bought Allison's necklace, but none of them were the right fit for my girl. I make my way to the end of the case, and that's when I see it, the perfect ring for Allison. It's a one carat princess cut diamond with baguettes interlaced down each side, tightly woven. I have been looking online for the last few weeks getting an idea of what's out there and what I think Allie would like. I ask the sales lady, who has been hovering over me, if I can see it. I examine it in my hands, it's perfect. I feel Aiden come up beside me, and he whistles.

"Holy shit, are you going to propose?" he asks, shocked.

I shrug my shoulders. "Well, yeah. I love her." I hand the ring back to the sales lady. "I'll take it in a size six, please." I turn back to Aiden. "I have my trust money Hales and I got when Granddad passed, I've never touched it until now." I smile at him. "Do you think she's going to like it?"

"Yeah, man, I do. It looks like Allison," he agrees.

I pay for Allison's ring, Aiden finishes up his shopping, and we start home. We pull into his driveway, and I hand him the bag from the jewelry store. "Keep this for me, man. I can't hide it in our luggage." He smiles and shakes his head.

The next few days fly by. This is mainly due to the fact Allison allows me to sleep with her in her room. Hales sleeps over at Aiden's in the guest room. I make sure she is okay with it. She just smiles and tells me to enjoy my girl. My sister knows what Allison means to me, she also knows how cranky I get when I don't get to sleep with her in my arms.

Christmas Eve we have a huge brunch that Mrs. Emerson, along with Hailey and Allison, prepare. We eat way too much and open gifts. I brought half of Allie's gifts for her to open here. She got three outfits and her boots. She got me the new Call of Duty for the Xbox and an iTunes gift card. Aiden and Hales are exchanging gifts tomorrow.

After brunch and presents, Allison wants to go visit her parents' grave. I beg her to let me go with her, but she says she needs to go alone. She does agree to let Hales drive her. I am relieved that at least she won't be driving upset. Aiden went to hang out with his parents, and I stay with Gran. We sit, talking for a while, and I suddenly have the urge to show her the ring. I text Aiden and ask him if he could bring it over. Before I know it, he's walking in the room with a grin on his face.

I take a seat in the chair beside Gran. "I want you to know I love Allison with everything in me. I would like to have your permission to marry her." I open the ring box and lay it in her hands.

"Oh, Liam, it's beautiful." Gran takes the ring out of the box and examines it. "This is perfect for Allison, you know her so well." She replaces the ring in the box and hands it back to me, grasping my hand. "Liam, I'm honored that you asked for my permission. Allison loves you so much, and you make her so happy. You've brought life back to my girl. You've already promised me to always take care of her, so, of course, you have my blessing to marry her."

I kiss her on the cheek. "Thank you, I promise she'll always be loved and protected, you have my word." I hand the ring back to Aiden. He shoves it into his pocket and takes it back to his house.

CHAPTER THIRTY-ONE

Allison

I AGREE to let Hailey drive me to the cemetery, more for Liam's piece of mind. I know he really wants to be here with me, but I need to talk to my parents about him. I know that sounds odd, but losing them at such a young age, growing up without them, and coming here and talking to them about life always seemed to help. Hailey eases into the cemetery lot and turns off Liam's Pathfinder. "I'll be right here if you need me," she says as she squeezes my hand.

I squeeze hers back. "Thank you for being here, for doing this."

"Anytime, but promise me you won't shut Liam out, he loves you and wants to be there for you."

"I know, and I love him too, so much. When I was little I would come here and talk to my parents about everything and, well, I kind of want to tell them about Liam." I slip my gloves onto my hands. "I know you're his sister, but you've also become my best friend. Liam, he says he wants forever with me. I know we're young and haven't been together all that long, but I want that too." I watch her closely studying her reaction.

Hailey grins. "So, what you're saying is that we're going to be sisters?"

I laugh. "Hopefully, one day."

"Allison, if Liam told you he wanted forever, he means it. You're it for him."

I reach over and give her a hug. "I won't be long." I get out of the truck and make my way to my parents' graves. Sadly, this is a path I've travelled many times the last eight years. I lay the fresh flowers we stopped for on the way here at the base of their headstone. "Hey, guys, I've missed you. College is good. I've met some amazing people. Aiden's there, and, well, I've kinda fallen head over heels for his room-mate. Funny thing is, my roommate Hailey is Aiden's roommate's sister. Small world, I know. His name is Liam, and he's amazing. He's tall, dark, and handsome, Mom. I know you would approve. Dad, he's the quarterback for the football team, and rumor has it he and Aiden are going to be first round draft picks for the NFL. He's so good to me, Daddy. He treats me like I'm the most precious gift in his life. Things are serious between us. He wanted to come with me today to meet you, but I wanted to be able to tell you about him first. I love him so much, he's my future, and, well, I just wanted you to know I'm okay. I'm living life and missing you every day, but I'm slowly painting my canvas as Gran would say. I need to get going, sorry I can't stay long. Aiden and Liam are waiting for us at Gran's. We're heading to Liam and Hailey's parents' for Christmas. His parents are wonderful and already treat me as if I'm a member of the family. I love you both and miss you every single day. Merry Christmas." I kiss my fingers and place them over their headstone, wipe the tears from my eyes, then turn and walk away.

I climb back into the Pathfinder, wiping the stray tears from my eyes. Hailey reaches over and grabs my hand, silently offering me support. By the time we make it back to Gran's, my tears are under control, that is, until Liam comes barrelling out of the house. He must have heard us pull up. He runs to my side, just as I'm stepping out. He captures me in one of his hugs, and I feel the dam break. Tears flood my eyes, and I sob into his chest. Tears of sadness and tears of happiness combined. Liam picks me up, bridal style, and carries me to the porch swing. He sits down with me on his lap, holding me tight.

He places a kiss on the top of my head as he softly whispers, "I love you." He doesn't say anything else. He just holds me close and lets me cry. After several minutes, I'm able to control my tears. "How you feeling?" he asks me.

I sit up on his lap. "Good, I'm sorry you had to see that."

Liam tucks my hair behind my ear. "Don't apologize, I want all of you, Allison, anyway I can get you." He kisses my temple. "Do you want to talk about it?"

"I wanted to tell my parents about you. I wanted to tell them I had fallen head over heels in love with you." I reach up and press my palm against his cheek. "My tears are happy and sad. Happy I have you in my life, that I have you to wrap your arms around me and make me feel safe. Sad, they will never get to meet you and see how amazing you are. They'll never get to see the happiness you've given me." I take a deep breath. "When you came rushing out the door to me, I couldn't control my emotions anymore," I explain.

"They're always with you, with us. They know how much I love you." He holds me tighter, and when he speaks again, I can hear the emotion in his voice. "They know you're my forever."

It's getting late, so we say goodbye to Gran and Aiden's parents and begin the journey to the MacCoys'. Liam and Aiden load the Pathfinder, and Liam tosses Aiden his keys. Aiden nods his head, understanding Liam wants to sit in the back with me. He tucks me close under his arm. I'm emotionally exhausted and fall fast asleep in his arms.

I wake up to Liam pressing a kiss to my forehead. "Wake up, baby, we made it." I open my eyes and smile at him.

"I love you, Liam MacCoy," I whisper in my husky sleep laced voice. I'm gifted with his smile, dimples and all.

"I love you too, beautiful. Let's get you inside."

Exhausted from the long day we say a quick hello to Mr. and Mrs. Mac and turn in. I quickly change into one of Liam's t-shirts and slide into bed. As I slide in Liam reaches for me. He draws me tight against his chest. "Goodnight, beautiful. I love you." I manage to tell him I love him too before falling back to sleep.

Christmas morning with the MacCoys is amazing. We all sit in the living room eating pastries and drinking coffee before opening gifts. I'm nervous to give Liam the gift I made him, so I busy myself with passing out my gifts to everyone else. Mr. and Mrs. Mac love the gift card Aiden and I got them to a restaurant close to the bed and breakfast Liam and Hailey reserved for them. Aiden loves his Best Buy gift card. He wants a new stereo system for his car. Hailey squeals when she opens her Coach wristlet and matching iPhone case. I smile shyly at Liam as I hand him his gift. He smiles at me in return and hands me two more as well. He, of course, makes me go first.

I open the larger one first and grin from ear to ear when I see it's the new Coach purse I've been eyeing at Macy's. "Go on, you've got one more." Liam urges me. I slowly un-wrap the last gift and open the black felt case. Nestled inside is a beautiful diamond heart necklace. I look up at Liam with tears in my eyes. "I figured since you own my heart you should have a symbol of it to wear as well," he says while his entire family and Aiden watch us.

I don't care who's watching, I launch myself at him and hug him tight. "Thank you, Liam. I love it. It's beautiful."

"Not as beautiful as you," he whispers so only I can hear. He clasps the delicate chain around my neck, placing a soft kiss against my nape when he's done. I grab the box that his last gift is in and hand it to him. *Here goes nothing.* Liam makes quick work of the wrapping paper and gently lifts the lid off of the box. He pulls out the pale blue book that represents our school colors. Liam opens the book, and then looks back at me. "How did you?" He turns to the next page. "Where did you?" He looks through a few more pages, before setting the book aside and capturing me in a soul searing kiss. "I love it, and I love you. This is the most amazing gift ever. When did you find the time to do this?"

I sigh with relief that he likes it. "I worked on it the weekends you had away games and spent at Gran's. She gets tired easy these days and sleeps a lot, so I worked on it while she napped."

"What is it?" Aiden asks him. I kept the gift a secret from him.

Liam smiles as he passes it to him. "It's a scrapbook of my entire football career," he tells him as he reaches for me and gives me one of his bear hugs. "You're amazing, Allison." The book is passed around, and everyone compliments me on it. Once they've all looked at it, Liam sits on the floor between my legs and studies the details of every page. I explain to him that his mom and Hailey both helped me with pictures. I included his pee wee days all through college.

"Well, there's just one more gift to give," Mr. Mac says as he gets up and grabs four envelopes from the mantel. "We know how close all of you are, and well, we thought it might be nice if all of you were able to get away for a weekend." He hands each of us an envelope. "All of these are the exact same, but we wanted each of you to be able to open one, so on the count of three." On three we all tear open our envelopes, and inside is a voucher for a three-night stay at a log cabin in Gatlinburg, Tennessee. All four of us are immediately on our feet, hugging Mr. and Mrs. Mac and thanking them for the gift. "There's no expiration date, and it's paid in full, so you guys can go when you can get your schedules to mesh. Of course, you'll have to call to schedule your date with the company."

We're only able to stay at Liam's parents for two days due to Liam and Aiden needing to get back for football practice. They're playing in a bowl game on New Year's Day.

Liam unloads all of our gifts into our room while I unload all of the leftovers Mrs. Mac sent home with us. Once I am done, I walk back to the bedroom and find Liam sitting on the bed, propped up against the headboard, looking through his scrapbook in his lap. "Hey."

"This really is incredible, Allison," he says as he continues to flip through the pages. "You managed to capture my entire football career in this book. This means so much to me. This is the most personal gift I've ever been given, and to know you made it for me, makes it even better."

"I wanted to do something special for you." I hesitate. I am afraid to tell him what I am thinking. I decide to just go for it, he loves me. "I thought it would be something you could show your kids one day." I shrug.

He leans over and kisses me softly on the lips. "I will definitely be showing this to *our* kids, so they can see how amazingly talented their mom is."

CHAPTER THIRTY-TWO

Liam

WAKING up with Allison tangled in my arms is something I'll never get tired of. She pretty much lives here now. Well, not technically, but most of her clothes are here, as well as all of her books and laptop. It's been weeks since she's stayed at her dorm. Hailey's always here too, unless she has a date, which has been less often. The four of us have become a tight knit group. Allison thinks there might be something brewing with Aiden and Hailey, but I don't see it. Of course, I rarely pay attention to anything else when Allison is around, I'm captivated by her.

Today is New Year's Eve Eve, and since Aiden and I have a big game New Year's Day and we fly out to Miami tomorrow, we decide to just have a quiet night at the apartment. Hailey decides to stay in with us, as well as Blitzen and his date, Jerrica. Blitzen very seldom has dates, he's more of a hook-up kind of guy. I can't judge him, because I used to be the same way before Allie. Maybe Jerrica will be the one to help him change his ways.

Hailey and Allison take care of all of the food preparation while Aiden and I set up the living room to accommodate everyone. We picked up a case of beer, but that's all since we have practice and a flight tomorrow. Tonight, we're just going to chill, not get our drink on. Hell, all I want to do is make love to Allison, but what else is new.

When Blitzen and Jerrica arrive, you can tell she feels out of place, being the only new person to the group. Allison must sense this, because she quickly introduces herself and drags Jerrica off to the kitchen with her and Hales.

"So, you ready for the big game?" Blitzen asks us.

"We got this," Aiden replies as he holds a fist out to each of us to bump.

"I think our chances are good, our team is strong," I respond. We continue to talk about the game until the girls get our attention by yelling that the food's ready, didn't have to tell us twice. They have really outdone themselves. We have meatballs, buffalo chicken dip, finger sandwiches, chips, cookies, and brownies.

I tug Allison to my chest and kiss her just below her ear. "Thank you for doing all this."

She smiles as she turns to Jerrica, trying to include her. "Thanks again for helping us get all of this together," she tells her.

"This is so good," Aiden says as he shoves a meatball in his mouth. I watch while Hailey grabs a napkin and wipes his face for him. *Interesting.*

After we eat, we gather in the living room for a game of battle of the sexes. The girls kick our asses. So, of course, us being the manly men that we are, we refuse to play again and demand another game. We vote for Rock Band, so we take turns, guys and girls. Of course, we're all acting crazy and making fun of each other, which leads to cranking up the iPod and dancing around the living room. Aiden, Blitzen, and I decide it is time for more food. Once we return to the living room, the girls have cleaned up the games and are starting a movie. We're watching Easy A, and surprisingly none of us have seen it before. I sit down in the recliner and tug Allison down on top of me. Blitzen and Jerrica take the love seat while Aiden and Hailey take the couch. The movie is good, at least what I watch of it. It is hard to focus with Allison's warm body snuggled up against me. The movie ends right before midnight, which works out so we're all able to get our New Year's kiss. I'm able to see Aiden pulling back from Hailey as I pull my lips away from Allison's. I know he wouldn't hurt her, and I can't exactly tell him to keep his hands off my little sister, since Allison is just like a sister to him and I pursued her. I'll have to at least mention it, another time though.

Blitzen and Jerrica thank us for having them and leave a short time later. Allison and I say goodnight to Hales and Aiden, and lock ourselves in our room. We go through what has now become our routine, brushing our teeth together and changing for bed. Allison crawls into her side of the bed and I follow, pulling her next to me as close as I can get her. *She's never close enough.*

"I love you, beautiful girl," I whisper in her ear.

She looks over her shoulder. "I love you too, Liam."

I kiss her. She rolls over to face me and deepens the kiss. I have my hand on her thigh and slowly move it up under my t-shirt she's wearing to cup her breast. The next thing I know, she has her shirt off and is pulling at my boxer briefs. I take the hint and make quick work of taking them off and throwing them on the floor. Allison climbs on top of me and continues our tongue duel. She pulls back and gently guides me home. I immediately sit up and hug her. I kiss her neck and work my way down to her breasts, slowly making love to them with my tongue. Allison must have different plans as she pushes me back onto the bed and begins to rock against me. My hands find her hips, and I assist her with bringing us both the pleasure we crave. I'm so close, and I want us to fall over the edge together, so I gently rub between her thighs. This brings us both crashing into bliss within mere seconds. She collapses on top of me, and I instantly wrap my arms around her and kiss the top of her head.

My mind travels to the engagement ring I have hidden in Aiden's room. I know now isn't the right time, but soon. I have to know I'll have these moments with her forever. I need to make her mine in every way.

Allison pulls herself off of me, and immediately I miss the connection, the warmth of being inside of her. She curls up on her side and wiggles back against my chest, where she belongs. It's only a matter of minutes until I feel her completely relax and her breathing evens out, so I know she's asleep. I gently brush her hair back from her ear and whisper, "I love you, Allie, so much. I can't wait to marry you." And then sleep takes over.

CHAPTER THIRTY-THREE

Allison

I WAKE up alone and look at the hotel clock. It's ten. The guys had to be at the field at nine-thirty. Kick-off is at twelve-thirty. *I need to get a move on.* I faintly remember Liam kissing me goodbye, but nothing after that. I drag myself out of bed and hop in the shower. I throw on my favorite pair of Rock Revival jeans along with a long sleeve t-shirt underneath my MacCoy jersey. I straighten my hair and place my UNC hat on my head. The weatherman says it's going to be in the fifties today, so that should be plenty of clothing. The way Hailey and I jump around and cheer, we keep ourselves plenty warm. I venture down to the lobby and find Hailey ready to go, sporting the same jersey as me.

"Hey, you, are you ready to head out?" she asks me.

"Yes, Mr. and Mrs. Emerson are headed down as well. How about your parents?"

Hailey nods. "I just talked to Mom. She said they were walking onto the elevator, so they should all be here at the same time."

"Sounds good. I'm going to call Gran on the way and wish her a happy new year and check in." We gather our phones, keys, pocket some money in our jeans, you can't watch a purse when you're trying to focus on the game, lock the door and we are good to go.

Hailey's driving, so I hop into the passenger seat and pull out my phone to call Gran. "Hey, Judy," I say to her homecare nurse. "Can I talk to Gran?" I listen while Judy tells me that Gran wasn't feeling well this morning and is laying down for a nap. "Okay, well, when she wakes up tell her I called and I'll call her after the game." Judy agrees to relay my message, and we say goodbye. Pulling into the stadium, we spot Liam and Hailey's parents, as well as Aiden's, waiting for us by the entrance. We all enter together and take our seats. Liam being the quarterback has its advantages, he has scored us the same seats all season.

The game is awesome. We're in the fourth quarter, one minute to go, and we're up two touchdowns. Hailey and I have been on our feet the entire game. I feel my phone vibrate in my back pocket, I pull it out to check it and see it's Grans' number. It's so loud in the stadium I'll never be able to hear her and there are only a few minutes left, so I hit ignore with the intentions of calling her back as soon as the game is over. I hope to relay a win, maybe she's watching at home as well. She and I have watched all of the away games together. Gran quickly became addicted to watching football. I smile, remembering her yelling at the television one Saturday when Liam got sacked. She was so not impressed.

Not thirty seconds later I feel my pocket vibrate again, I pull out my phone and see it's Judy, Gran's homecare nurse. I glance at the scoreboard and there's nineteen seconds left in the game, we have the ball and are still up by two touchdowns. I bump Hailey's shoulder and tell her gran tried to call and now Judy is trying too, so I'm going to head out of the stands and call them back just to make sure everything is okay. I make it out of the stands to the landing by a concession stand, which has already closed, so there aren't a lot of people around. I pull out my phone and hit redial for Judy.

"Hey, Judy, it's Allison, sorry I couldn't take your call. It's crazy loud in here, and I couldn't hear. What's up?" I ask her.

"Allison," Judy chokes and my heart drops.

"Judy. What's wrong?" I ask, fear lacing my voice.

"I'm so sorry, sweetie, she was sleeping, and I went to check on her and—and—" She's crying now, and I can't find my words to coach her to continue to just spit it the fuck out, to tell me what happened. "She—she wasn't breathing. I tried to do CPR, but it was too late, she was already gone."

My body is taken over by wrenching sobs as pain laces through me, and the tears flow heavily down my cheeks. "No," I sob into the phone.

"Allison, I am so sorry to tell you this way, but I knew you would want to know." She sniffles into the phone. "Allison, the funeral home just showed up, so I need to go. I'll call you back as soon as this is all situated," she tells me.

"I...I'm on my way. I will be there as soon as I can," I tell her as I hit end on my phone. I'm crying so hard my chest is heaving with sobs, without thinking I take off running toward the parking lot. Gran. I need to get there as fast as I can. Through my tears, my vision is blurry, and I'm not watching where I'm going when I feel myself bump into someone. I look up and see Jason and this makes me cry even harder. I don't need to deal with this asshole right now. What is he doing here anyway?

Jason gently grabs my arm to keep me from falling. I see his arm is still in a cast. Serves him right. "Slow down, Allison, what's wrong?" he asks me. I'm surprised he even asked.

Instead of answering him, I back up into the wall, letting my body rest against it, and let the tears flow.

"Allison, you're scaring me. Where's Liam, do you need me to find him for you?" His voice is laced with concern.

I nod, unable to speak through the tears. Jason puts his arm around me as he pulls his phone out of his pocket. "Okay, can you tell me his number?" I shake my head, but hold out my hand that has my cell phone in it. He takes it and starts to scroll through to find Liam's number.

Before he even gets a chance to hit send I hear Liam's deep voice. "What the fuck did you do to her? I'm going to fucking kill you this time!" he yells as he plows toward us, flanked by security guards. He's still in his uniform, sans helmet and shoulder pads. The look on his face is pure rage, however, the rage doesn't register with me. All I see is Liam, the man I love, and I need to be in his arms, I need him wrapped around me. I push myself off the wall, and run and launch myself at him. He immediately lifts me up, and I wrap my legs around his waist and my arms around his neck, squeezing him tight. Liam's whispering in my ear, "I got you, beautiful, you're safe." He kisses my neck. "What happened, baby?"

I hear Aiden. "You're going to have more than a broken arm by the time I'm through with you!" he roars as he stalks his way toward Jason. It's then I realize I need to stop this. Jason was trying to help me, help me get to Liam.

"Aiden, no!" I scream, and he stops in his tracks. I release my legs from the hold they have on Liam, and he gently sets me back on my feet, keeping me tucked close to his side. I'm still crying, but the sobs ease just a little when I feel Liam tighten his hold on me.

"Jason—he was—he was helping me." I start to cry harder. "He was calling Liam for me." As proof of what I was saying he hands Liam my cell phone.

"Here, man, she ran into me and she was crying so hard, she couldn't even see where she was going. I asked her if she needed help and she nodded her head. I asked her if I could call you for her, but she couldn't tell me your number she was so upset. Instead, she handed me her cell phone. I was just getting ready to call you."

I nod my head, agreeing to what Jason is telling them. Liam bends his knees and uses his finger to lift my chin, so I'm looking at him. "Allie, baby, what happened? Did someone hurt you?" I can see the tension in his jaw at the mere thought that someone has hurt me.

I shake my head. Aiden rubs his hands up and down my back,

while his parents stand close by, but I refuse to let go of Liam. I tighten my arms around him, take a deep breath, and rasp out the words, "She's gone."

"Who's gone?" he asks, still keeping an eye on Jason.

All of them look really confused except for Hailey. She knew I was going out to return a call to Judy. "Oh, God," she cries.

"What? Can someone, please, tell me what is going on?" Liam raises his voice. I tense at the sound. "I'm sorry, baby, I'm scared. I don't know what's wrong, you're upset, and I can't make it go away unless you tell me," he pleads.

"Gran, she's g...g...gone. J...Judy..." I break down in sobs. "Judy called, she was sleeping, she checked on her, and she's gone. She tried CPR, but it was too late, she was already gone." I bury my head in Liam's chest and let the pain that is tearing through my heart unleash with my tears.

He squeezes me tight. "Oh, Allie, I'm so sorry." He embraces me in his arms. "I'm taking her home," he says to everyone.

"No, I need to go to her. I need to go to Grans. Please." I cry harder.

"Okay, I'll take you there." He looks to Aiden. "Can you get my bag from the locker room and meet us at the car? I have a change of clothes in there I can change into when we get there."

"Sure, man, go on, and I'll be right behind you," Aiden says, already turning in the direction of the locker room.

"Dad, can you call the airport and get us on the next flight out?"

"I got it covered, son," he tells Liam.

"I'm coming with you," Hailey says to Aiden as she follows him.

"Allison, honey." Mrs. Emerson is rubbing my back. "We're changing our flight as well. We'll meet you there, okay, sweetheart?"

I nod, but it's Liam who responds, "Thank you both. Mom, Dad, I'll call you and keep you posted."

"Sounds good, son, you just take care of our girl," Liam's dad tells him. Both of his parents give me a hug. I still refuse to let go of Liam.

He turns to Jason. "Thanks, man, for helping her."

Jason nods. "I'm sorry for your loss, Allison." Then he walks away.

Liam picks me up and carries me out to the cab that's waiting to take us back to the hotel. He opens the rear passenger door to set me in the car, and I panic. I keep my hold firm around his neck. "Oh, Allison, baby, I'm so sorry," he says, tightening his grip on me.

I hear Aiden talking and the next thing I know Liam's climbing in the back seat with me in his arms, never letting me go. He holds me close and continues to tell me how sorry he is, how much he loves me, and how everything is going to be okay.

All I can think is I'm alone, all alone. I have no family left in the world. It's just me. I feel hollow inside. My tears continue to flow as I fall asleep in Liam's arms.

CHAPTER THIRTY-FOUR

Liam

MY FUCKING HEART IS BREAKING. Allison refuses to let go of me, so I'm holding her in my arms while Aiden drives us to Gran's from the airport. My beautiful girl is in so much pain, and I don't know what to do to make it better. She falls asleep almost instantly, and I'm glad. She has an emotional journey ahead of her, and I need a minute to get my emotions in check. I went from elation from the win, to full on outrage, to scared shitless, to heartbroken for her. That's a damn tornado of emotions in a span of what, five minutes. When I thought Jason had hurt her, I was going to kill him. I wouldn't have stopped until he was dead. Then when she told me he was helping her, fear crashed through me, who hurt her? What happened to have her this upset? When she finally told me Gran was gone, I felt my heart breaking. Not only had I become close to Gran over the last several months, but I knew what this meant for Allison. The devastation of losing Gran is going to take a toll on her emotionally, and I have no fucking idea how to help her.

We pull into the driveway, and Allison is still asleep. She slept the entire flight as well. I brush the hair off her cheek and whisper in her ear, "Allie, we're here. Wake up."

She bolts straight up in the seat, flings the door open, and runs to the house. It takes my brain about ten seconds to register before I'm right behind her. I catch up to her as she's going up the steps. I reach around her and open the door. Judy's sitting in the living room, curled up on the couch with a box of tissues. The chair where Gran always sits is empty. Allison starts to fall to her knees, but I catch her just in time. I lower us both to the floor and cradle her in my lap while her entire body shakes with gut wrenching sobs. Her tears are falling so fast, I can't wipe them away. I feel tightness in my chest and before I even realize it, I'm crying too. I want to take this pain from her, I want to make it better, and I can't. I'm scared to death for her, for how this is going to affect her emotionally. God, how am I going to get her through this?

Aiden and Hailey come in, carrying our bags. Aiden's parents are right behind them. Aiden has showered and changed. "Ash," Aiden says, "come sit with me, let's let Liam get showered and changed." He speaks softly to her. We left the game, the celebration and went straight to the hotel to pack and then to the airport. Dad was able to get the four of us a flight within a few hours of finding out about Gran. Showering was the last thing I was thinking about, but I did manage to change out of my uniform before Allie was latched back onto me. *My girl is broken.*

Allison shakes her head. "Can I—can I come with you?" she asks me.

"I can wait, baby, we're good here for now," I tell her.

"No, you need to shower and change, but I just…"

"Allison," Mrs. Emerson addresses her, "how about you and I take a walk?"

She hesitates before looking at me with sad worried eyes. "A walk might do you some good," I tell her.

"Will you be here when I get back?" she questions me.

I crush her tighter to my chest. "I'm not going anywhere, beautiful girl. I'll shower and be here waiting when you get back."

"Promise?" she whispers.

I swallow the lump in my throat. "I promise." With that she allows Mrs. Emerson to help her up, and they leave out the front door to take a walk. I pull my legs to my chest and rest my elbows on my knees with both hands covering my eyes. She was afraid I would leave her. *Oh, Allie.*

I feel Aiden place his hand on my shoulder. "You alright, man?"

"No," my voice is deep and thick with emotion, "I can't help her. I can't take this pain away and it's killing me. She's my world, and I can't protect her from this. She was afraid I was going to leave her." I look up and meet his stare. "My beautiful girl is broken, and fuck if I know how to fix her."

"She needs you, man, she was clinging to you like you were her lifeline. Just be there for her, hold her. She'll get through this, we all will. Go take a shower. Dad's going to pick up some dinner."

I rush through my shower, because I want to be finished when Allison gets back from her walk. I make my way back to the living room to find Judy still sitting there by herself. I kneel down in front of her. "You okay? Can I get you anything?" I ask her.

"No, thank you. I'm going to head home as soon as Allison returns," she says solemnly.

I hear the front door open and turn to see Allison, Hailey, and Mrs. Emerson returning from their walk. Allison walks straight toward me, so I open my arms for her. I kiss the top of her head, but don't say anything. I know nothing I say can take her pain away.

"Thanks for being here, Judy, and taking care of everything," Allison says, her voice cracking.

"Oh, sweetie, you're welcome. I'm going to head home now, but I'll be back to check in on you tomorrow. I left some paperwork there on the table, letters, copies of her will, that kind of thing." Judy stands to leave. "You call me if you need anything, sweet girl. We'll get through this."

Allison turns, buries her face in my chest, and wraps her arms around my waist and squeezes. I hold her tight, hoping I'm relaying to her that I'm here for whatever she needs. We stand like this for I don't know how long, when finally, she asks me to sit down with her. We make our way to the couch. She pushes me down and sits on my lap, curling up against me. I gently stroke her back. I point to the table. "There's the stack of papers Judy left you. Do you need me to sort through them for you?" I volunteer. Before she can answer, Hailey walks in to tell us everything is set up for dinner.

"Let's get you something to eat," I suggest.

"I'm not really hungry."

"I know, babe, but you need to keep your strength up. You have a tough couple of days ahead of you. Can you just try to eat a little, please?"

She nods. Hailey was apparently listening, because she suddenly appears with two plates loaded down. Aiden follows with drinks. Allison starts to get up. "You can stay right where you are, baby, you don't need to move." She releases a deep breath.

"Thank you, Liam," she speaks softly. "I love you." Her voice breaks with emotion on the last words, and I'll be damned but do I tear up again.

"I love you so much, Allie. We will get through this." I kiss her cheek, and we both pick at our food, neither of us has an appetite. I increase my effort, just so I can try to convince her to do the same.

We finish picking at our plates when Aiden's parents come in to tell us goodnight. They offer for all four of us to sleep at their place tonight. Allison thanks them, but says that she wants to stay here tonight. I'm going to be where she is, no matter where that happens to be.

Aiden and Hailey stick around until about eleven. They both offer to stay the night, and Aiden offers his house again, Allison declines. I don't bother to respond, they both know I am with her, no matter where she chooses to sleep.

CHAPTER THIRTY-FIVE

Allison

AIDEN AND HAILEY leave to go to Aiden's for the night, which leaves Liam and I all alone in Gran's house. I suddenly realize maybe Liam doesn't want to stay here. "Liam, you can stay at Aiden's if you would rather."

"Nope, wherever you are is where I want to be," he says as he kisses my forehead.

"Thank you." I take a deep breath. "I guess I need to look through the paperwork Judy left," I say, pointing to the stack on the table.

"We don't have to do that tonight, babe. We can just leave it all for tomorrow and try to get some rest tonight."

"I don't think I could sleep now, even if I wanted to. Will you go through it with me?" I ask him. I know I'm leaning on him for pretty much everything, but he calms me.

"Anything you need," he tells me. He's being so amazing through all of this. I sit down on the floor between Liam's legs and begin sifting through the stack of papers. There's a copy of Gran's will, which outlines that she has already planned and paid for her funeral, when the time come. She's to be buried in the same cemetery as my parents and grandpa. The house and all of her remaining assets are left to me. The house is paid for, so there's no mortgage to worry about.

"This gives you time to go through her belongings and decide what you want to do with the house and everything else without the pressure of a mortgage." Liam's trying his hardest to help me stay sane. I love him.

The stack also contains the deed to the house, as well as all her banking information she had already listed me on so there would be no issues with having it tied up in probate court. There's an addendum in the will explaining where I can find documents such as my parents' marriage license, birth certificates, etc. Gran had apparently kept all of it when we sold the house after they died, just in case I would want it someday. Tears prick my eyes, I miss her so much already, and it hasn't even been a day.

Liam's gently massaging my shoulders while I work my way through the stack of documents. Occasionally, he'll lean down and kiss the top of my head. I don't even want to think about how this day would have been without him here. I suddenly realize I forgot to congratulate him on his win today. I look over my shoulder at him. "Congrats on your win. I'm sorry I forgot to tell you."

"Hey," he says, moving all my hair from one shoulder to the other. "You have nothing to be sorry for." He leans down and kisses my cheek. I smile weakly and turn back to the task of sifting through the mound of paperwork. Really, it isn't a mound, just a small stack, but the heaviness it brings to my heart makes it look like a damn mountain.

I've finally worked my way to the bottom of the stack and find an envelope with my name written on it. I suck in a breath and feel the tears start to slide down my cheeks. Liam puts his hands under my arms and lifts me onto his lap and engulfs me in a hug. A hug so loving and full of emotion, one that only Liam can give. "You don't have to read it now."

Logically, I know he's right, I can put it aside and call it a night. However, my heart knows these are her final words to me, and even though I know it's going to shatter my heart, I want to read it. I want to know what she felt was important enough to transcribe into words on paper, knowing she was leaving me.

Liam's rubbing soothing circles on my back. I sit up to face him. "I need to know." I slide the envelope open and pull out the letter. I rest my head against his chest, preparing myself for the onslaught of emotion that's sure to consume me because of the piece of paper in my hand.

Allie Girl-

Since you're reading this, you already know I took care of all of the funeral arrangements, and you should have received all important documents, or at least know where to find them. Everything is yours now, Allie. I don't want you to feel obligated to keep the house. I want you to do what is best for you. Home is where your heart is.

I want you to know how much I love you. You've brought so much joy to my life. I'm so proud of the young woman you've become, and I know your parents would be proud of you as well. It saddens me to know I won't be here to see you get married or become a mom. I'll be watching over you, and know I'll be with you every day in spirit. Each time life throws you something new, good and bad, I will be there.

You've found yourself a fine young man to spend your life with. Let him love you, Allie. Paint your canvas full of vibrant colors and enjoy the laughter and love life brings you. I have your past, but Liam has your future. Don't be afraid to give your whole heart. Live and love fearlessly.

I'll always be with you. I love you, Allie Girl.
Gran

. . .

I LET the letter fall to my lap as my body heaves with sobs. Liam holds me tighter. He doesn't speak, but then again, he doesn't have to. He knows I just need to process the emotions racing through me. We sit like this for what feels like hours. Finally, I reach for the letter and hand it to him, so he can read it himself. He shakes his head slightly. "I read it over your shoulder, baby." Kissing the top of my head. "I do, you know." I look up at him in question. "I love you like a bee loves honey." I chuckle, I can't help it. He's obviously trying to lighten the mood and it works. He always seems to know what I need.

I stand up, pulling him with me, leading him down the hallway to my bedroom. Exhaustion is taking over and all I want to do is fall asleep in his arms. After changing for bed, brushing my teeth, and washing my tear-stained face I crawl into my bed beside Liam. Of course, he doesn't disappoint as he draws my back against his chest and secures his arms around me. I faintly hear him telling me he loves me as the exhaustion seizes me.

The next few days are nothing but a blur. Since Gran had everything planned and paid for, all we had to do was wait for the minister to be available. Since Gran and I have no other family, I settle for a small graveside service. Liam's parents are here with Hailey, as well as Aiden and his parents. Judy and her husband are here and a few ladies from her church. That's it, small and simple. We lay Gran to rest with Judy singing Amazing Grace.

CHAPTER THIRTY-SIX

Liam

THE WEEKS FOLLOWING the funeral are tough for Allison. My beautiful girl is heartbroken. We all rally around her, giving her support the best we know how. It's almost as if she's just going through the motions to get through each day. Hailey suggests that since spring break is coming up we should try to schedule our Gatlinburg vacation. We all agree the trip might do Allison some good. Aiden and I are also excited, because it's right before the draft, and we're both nervous as hell. Add in school wrapping up and worrying about Allison—we're all pretty stressed.

Allison agrees to the trip, just like we knew she would. Hailey calls and gets everything scheduled for the weekend leading into spring break. I'm nervous, yet excited to get away. I want my happy full of life Allison back. I don't know what to do for her. I know she needs to grieve, but she also needs to live. I've found her reading the letter her gran left her several times. She has read it so much the sheet is starting to wear at the creases.

The trip to Gatlinburg is nice, the weather is good, and the company even better. Hailey sits in the back with Allison and gets her singing along with the radio. I actually catch a real smile in the rearview mirror, and I make a mental note to do something really nice for my little sister. The cabin we're staying in is beautiful. It's a three bedroom, a pool, hot tub, and game room. My parents have really out done themselves.

The first night we decide to go into town and have dinner at the Hard Rock Café. After dinner, we're walking downtown, checking out the shops when we come upon a tattoo parlor. Our freshman year of college Aiden and I got wasted and ended up getting matching tribal tattoos on our biceps. I've been thinking about adding to mine and so has Aiden. We walk into the parlor and speak to the guy at the desk. He immediately starts working on the designs we have in mind. I feel Allison walk up beside me. "What do you think, beautiful, you like it?"

She smiles widely, nodding her head yes. "I want one too."

This is the first I've ever heard Allison mention being interested in getting ink. I throw my arm over her shoulder and tuck her close to my side. "What are you thinking about getting?"

"Well, actually I was thinking of getting script on the side of my foot."

"I'm digging it. What saying?"

"Live and love fearlessly," she replies softly.

I kiss the top of her head. "It's perfect." I've seen her read the letter from Gran enough times to know those are the words written in her letter. I can only hope this will help her heal. What started out as Aiden and me adding to our current tribal tats, turns into all four of us getting ink. Allison gets her script on the side of her foot, and it looks sexy as hell. Of course, anything on Allison is sexy as hell. Hailey ends up getting a fancy H on the top of her foot. Aiden and I both add the first letter of our last names to ours.

The tattoo seems to soothe something in Allison. Maybe she feels like Gran and her words will always be a part of her, but once we leave the tattoo parlor, my girl is back to normal. She's laughing and dancing in the street with Hailey, and I feel like I can breathe again. I hated seeing her in so much pain and not be able to do a fucking thing to make it better.

The rest of our stay is an absolute blast. During the day we hang out at the cabin, lounge around the pool, and play in the game room. At night we hit up the club scene in Gatlinburg, there's only one club, but the girls want to dance, so we dance. We laugh, dance, and drink the night away. We close down the club and continue our bash in the hot tub back at the cabin. Aiden and I also brought our guitars along, so we play and sing while the girls dance around the fire and sing along with us. When the day is done and we all retreat to our rooms, I make love to Allison.

Back home after the Gatlinburg trip, life is good. Allison's still sad at times, but her tattoo seems to help her in the grieving process. The draft is a few weeks away, and I have her engagement ring burning a hole in my pocket, or Aiden's drawer rather. Aiden and I have talked a lot about how and when. I didn't want to do it while she was still so deeply mourning Gran, but now she's doing better. She'd the old Allison, so I need to get my shit in gear and plan how I'm going to ask her to be my forever. I decide I definitely want to do it before the draft. I need assurance that no matter where I get drafted, if I do actually make the draft, she'll be with me.

Aiden and I are in meetings upon meetings with our coach and agents. *I have a fucking agent.* This is taking up a lot of our time, so taking Allison away for a night, even to the beach house, isn't in the cards. I have to improvise with a romantic setting at the apartment. I know I'll need help, more than just from Aiden, so I call in reinforcements, Mom and Hailey. After swearing Hales to secrecy, I'm able to tell them my plan and what I'll need from them to pull it off. It's the week before the draft, and I'm running out of time. I'm a nervous wreck for a multitude of reasons. Mom and Hailey are, of course, on board and over the moon that I'm asking Allison to marry me. Neither one of them were surprised I already had the ring, they were, however, surprised that it's been almost five months, and I still hadn't found the right time to ask her. I explain about not wanting to ask her too soon after Gran, because she was mourning. I want her to remember this as a happy time in our lives. A day we can tell our kids about, when we are old and gray. I know, I know, totally losing the man card, but love does that to you.

It's Wednesday, the day before we fly to New York for the NFL draft. Today's also the day that will determine my future, even more so than the draft. With Allison's schedule and mine, tonight is the only night I can get her in the apartment alone. Hailey's job is to take her out shopping and keep her away until seven o'clock. Mom, who also brought Dad with her, Aiden, and I get to work on the apartment. We re-arrange the living room furniture, so all the furniture is pressed against the wall. We throw scarfs over the lamps to dim the lighting and place extra-large throw pillows, which Mom picked up, on the floor for Allison and me to sit on. The kitchen is transformed to resemble a romantic restaurant with table cloth, candles, and daisies. Everything is perfect, so I say goodbye to my family as I rush through a shower. I dress in a pair of well-worn jeans and a plain white t-shirt. This is me, and I want her to just see me tonight, just Liam, the one who's madly in love with her.

My phone beeps, and I quickly read the text.

HAILEY: We just pulled in, good luck, big bro.

ME: Thank you.

GAME TIME and this is the biggest play yet. My nerves hit me hard, and I feel flutters in my stomach. *Oh, shit! What if she says no?* Just as I'm about to break out into full blown panic mode, I hear the handle on the door turn. I walk to the door to greet her, and as soon as I see her, my fears disappear. I love this girl, and I know she feels the same.

I lean in to kiss her lips. I'm afraid to get too close, afraid she'll feel her ring in my pocket. "Hey, beautiful." I take her bags and her purse and lay them down on the couch that's pushed next to the wall.

"Hey, what's all this?"

"This is me, having a romantic night with my girl. I've missed you. Things have been crazy, and with the draft starting tomorrow, I just need Allison time. You keep me calm." That's the truth, even though I'm leaving out the proposal. "Come on, I conned Mom into cooking for us. I wanted tonight to be special, so I didn't even attempt to do it on my own." At that, she laughs.

I lead her into the kitchen, and she gasps. "Liam, this is beautiful. I can't believe you did all of this."

Kissing her cheek, I pull out her chair. "You, my beautiful girl, deserve to be romanced."

I serve us lasagna and a bowl of salad, placing the bread sticks on the table. I sit down in the chair right next to hers. While we eat she talks about her day with Hailey, I admit I asked Hales to keep her out of the apartment, so I could set all this up. We decide to wait on dessert, so I lead her into the living room, and we sit down on the pillows in the middle of the floor. This is it, I reach for my guitar.

She smiles brightly. "You're going to play for me?"

I return her smile, even though my insides are shaking. "Yeah, I thought I would play something if that's okay?"

She nods, so I strum a few chords on my guitar before I begin to play "I Live My Life For You" by Firehouse. I belt out the lyrics, begging her to understand what she means to me. Once I finish the song, I stand and lean my guitar against the wall. I walk back to Allison, offer her my hand, and tug her to stand up with me. I gently wipe the tears from her cheeks with my thumbs.

"Allison, before you came crashing into my life I thought I knew what happiness was. I didn't think I needed love or someone by my side to share my moments with. Since meeting you, I've realized the moments are just that unless you share them with someone you love, that makes them memories. Memories filled with love, passion, sadness, laughs, and tears." I take a deep breath. "You, my beautiful girl, have captivated my heart and soul. You're my best friend, and I live my life for you. I don't want to live without you entwined in every aspect of my life. I love you." With that I get down on one knee and pull the ring out of my pocket. "Allison Shay Hagan, you are the air I breathe and blood in my veins. Will you be my forever, will you marry me?"

CHAPTER THIRTY-SEVEN

Allison

I CAN FEEL the crocodile tears rolling down my cheeks, and I'm unable to contain the smile I know is shining upon my face. I don't need to think about the answer as Gran's words flash through my mind. *'Let him love you, Allie.' 'Live and love fearlessly.'* I launch myself into his arms and crash my lips to his, kissing him with all the love inside of me. He pulls away, and I groan in protest. I bury my face in his neck breathing him in. Liam clears his throat.

"Um, is that a yes?" His voice is thick with emotion.

I lean back and grab his face with my hands. "That is a hell yes!" I crash my lips to his, opening my mouth, inviting him in. When we finally have to come up for air, Liam grabs my hand and slides the most beautiful ring I've ever seen into place. I look up at him, and then back to the ring. "Liam, it's beautiful."

Smiling he says, "That's what Gran said when I showed it to her."

I snap my head back to look at him. "W—what do you mean, when you showed it to her?"

"I bought the ring before Christmas. I showed it to Gran while we were there and asked her permission to ask you to be my wife. I had no idea that..." he trails off, not wanting to finish his sentence.

"She knew," I whisper.

"She's here with you, beautiful girl. She held the ring and said it was perfect for you. Aiden has been hiding it, because I was afraid you would find it in our room. I was just waiting for the right time to ask you. I knew it was you I wanted months ago, I just wanted the timing to be right."

I have so many emotions running through me. I'm elated Liam wants to spend the rest of his life with me. It's official, we're getting married. I'm stunned he's been holding onto the ring for months. I can't even describe what I'm feeling, knowing Gran saw my ring and she knew Liam was my forever. I'm sad for the fact Gran isn't physically here to see me marry the love of my life. Liam says she's here with us, and I have to believe he's right. She is here, watching over us.

Standing on my tiptoes, I press my lips to his. "I love you, Liam MacCoy," I speak softly against his lips.

"I love you too, future Mrs. MacCoy."

Liam's cell phone rings and he groans. He snatches it off the table he has pushed against the wall. "Somebody better be bleeding," he snarls, and I smack him on the arm. He gives me a look, letting me know he isn't impressed with the caller.

I can hear Hailey on the other end asking if he has asked me yet. Before he can reply, I pull the phone out of his hands. "I cannot believe you kept this from me," I tell her.

The reply I get is, "What did you say? Please tell me you said yes."

"Of course, I said yes!" Screaming commences on the other end of the line, and I have to pull the phone away from my ear.

Grinning, he takes it back from me and hangs up, not even bothering to tell her goodbye. "I should have known better than to answer." He lifts my hand to his mouth and kisses my ring.

"It's beautiful." I meet his gaze. "We're getting married."

"Hell, yes we are, but first I'm going to make love to my fiancée, then we're going to have dessert, then I'm going to make love to my fiancée again, and then we need to get some rest because tomorrow we fly to New York to determine our future."

"You should have waited to propose, I don't want this to take away from your excitement of the draft, you've worked hard to get where you are."

"Baby, I needed to know, before we leave here tomorrow, that no matter what happens you are with me forever and always. I don't care what team drafts me. Hell, if I don't get drafted so be it. The only thing that matters to me is I know that you, my beautiful girl, are my future, no matter what the outcome may be."

Again, with the damn tears. "I love you." I hug him tight.

"And I love you, so much."

EPILOGUE

Liam

I WOKE up this morning tangled up with my fiancée. She was sleeping peacefully in our mess of tangled limbs, her head resting on my chest. I kept her up later than I should have, but I couldn't help it. Making love to her knowing she'd agreed to marry me, well, let's just say once wasn't enough. This girl has changed me. I think back to the first time I saw her and I think deep down I knew then she was my game changer, although it took me weeks to admit it. Today is the big day, the NFL draft starts. Aiden and I are both rumoured to be first round picks; our agents say it's a done deal. A year ago, that was all I cared about. I would've been a nervous wreck going into this, but now holding this beautiful girl in my arms—I'm not nervous. Don't get me wrong, I've wanted this since I was old enough to hold a football, but holding her is more important. I know I have a good education to fall back on, and either way, I'll be able to provide for her. Granted, if I'm drafted I can not only take care of her, but spoil her to the degree of obscenity. Not that I need to. Allison's parents made sure she was set for life. That's her money though. I want to spoil her with mine. However, I know that's not what she wants or needs, she just wants me, and that's what keeps me calm. I know wherever we end up, she'll be there by my side.

I'm startled out of my thoughts when I hear Allison saying my name. "Liam." Damn, even her voice pulls me into her.

"Yeah, babe?"

"Your dad wants to know if you need anything, they're going to get drinks."

I look to my dad, who's grinning like he knows what I was thinking about. "No, thanks," I say as I lace my fingers with Allison's.

My agent, Tom, walks up. "Okay, Liam, they're about to start. Are you ready for this?"

I squeeze Allison's hand and kiss her temple. I turn to look at Aiden, who's sitting across the table from me, as well as his family and his agent. We insisted we all be together, that way we can celebrate. We've become one big family. I give Aiden a nod that he returns. "Let's do this."

We all watch from the screen as the announcer steps to the podium. "The North Carolina Panthers pick Liam MacCoy, quarterback, University of North Carolina." The table filled with my family and friends erupts with cheers.

I sit stunned until Allison takes my face in her hands. "You did it, babe!" She kisses me. "Go on, they're waiting for you." She pulls me to my feet and toward the stage. I walk out and receive my Panthers hat and jersey and get my picture taken with the head coach and the commissioner. We move off to the side to get family photos and once all of that is done we retreat back to our waiting room to determine Aiden's fate. On the way back to the room, I pull her aside, lift her off her feet, and crush my lips to hers. "We did it, baby, we made it to the big time!" She laughs and kisses me back. I hear cheers from our table, and see Aiden twirling Hales in circles. He puts her down and comes walking over wearing a grin. He walks straight to me and Allie and pulls us both into a bear crushing hug.

"Panthers, man. We're going to the same fucking team." He releases us and struts off toward the stage to do the same hat and jersey dance I'd just completed.

I rest my forehead against Allie's. "Looks like we're going to Charlotte, beautiful girl."

"I can plan a wedding in Charlotte."

What other response does that deserve other than a soul searing kiss, so that's what I give her. This amazing, beautiful, sexy creature is my future, and the Carolina Panthers just sweetened the deal.

THANK YOU

Thank you for taking the time to read Anywhere with You.

Read Aiden and Hailey's story now in More with You.
http://mybook.to/MoreWithYou

Never miss a new release:
http://bit.ly/31PaSoS

More about Kaylee's books:
http://bit.ly/2CV3hLx

Contact Kaylee Ryan:
Facebook: http://bit.ly/2C5DgdF
Instagram: http://bit.ly/2reBkrV
Reader Group: http://bit.ly/2oOyWDx
Goodreads: http://bit.ly/2HodJvx
BookBub: http://bit.ly/2KulVvH
Website: http://www.kayleeryan.com/

MORE FROM KAYLEE RYAN

With you Series:
*Anywhere with You | More with You
Everything with You*

Soul Serenade Series:
*Emphatic | Assured
Definite | Insistent*

Southern Heart Series:
*Southern Pleasure | Southern Desire
Southern Attraction | Southern Devotion*

Unexpected Arrivals Series
Unexpected Reality | Unexpected Fight

Standalone Titles:
Tempting Tatum | Unwrapping Tatum | Levitate

Just Say When | I Just Want You
Reminding Avery
Hey, Whiskey | When Sparks Collide
Pull You Through | Beyond the Bases
Remedy | The Difference
Trust the Push

Co-written with Lacey Black:

It's Not Over